Beautifully Played

Candied Crush #18

Charity Parkerson

Punk & Sissy Publications

Contents

♥

Introduction

♥

ENZO HAS A BIT of a hero complex. After meeting Aric, he may be the one who needs saving.

After leaving the Navy and moving back home to L.A., Enzo plans to work on himself. He's spent his life refusing to settle down. Now he's in his thirties and starting a new business. It looks like a good time to find something real and meaningful. When he rescues Aric from one of his handsy bar patrons, Enzo wonders if he's found what he's looking for.

There's no denying Enzo is gorgeous and tall, but Aric has been down this road before—literally. This is the second time Enzo has rescued him and then used him. Things are different this time around. Aric is older, and he knows a seducer when he sees one. He doesn't mind a little fun, but Enzo is the one who should take care. Aric doesn't intend to get played twice.

When Enzo's stubbornness meets Aric's bitterness, it's an explosion neither man can resist. Only time will tell if they can withstand the blast.

Chapter One

♥

IT WAS NIGHTS LIKE tonight that reminded Enzo of why he had changed careers. After ten years of serving in the Navy, Enzo had opened The Aviator. His initial plan had been to open a small bar with his twin and a friend of theirs geared toward the military crowd. A few things had happened since then, starting with his twin and their friend fucking him.

Enzo's twin, Marco, and their friend, Jake, had served in the Navy together since the beginning. Together, they had decided to retire, open a bar, and split the cost three ways. A few weeks before they were set to retire and move from San Diego to L.A., Marco and Jake changed their minds. They wanted to stay in the Navy. At first, Enzo had been angry and crushed. His brother had never let him down before. Then Enzo's younger brother, Tito, had married an angel, Cooper. Cooper was easily the most amazing person Enzo had ever met. At nineteen, he couldn't even drink yet, but he had the money to back Enzo. He hired a company to come up with a business model to help Enzo succeed. Then, for Enzo's thirty-second birthday, Cooper gifted him with a nightclub: The Aviator.

For the first time in Enzo's life, he lived without his twin and had money to burn. With Cooper's backing and shark lawyers, Enzo had become a huge success much faster than he ever dreamed. He was also lonelier than he had ever been. Life was just...

different. His whole life, he had been glued to his twin's side. Now they never saw each other. It was weird.

Stranger than living without Marco was his new job. Enzo had been born in L.A., but after living in San Diego for all his adult life, he didn't have any L.A. friends. Enzo had hoped this bar would help him meet new people. With Cooper's genius business model in place, Enzo wasn't needed at all at The Aviator. The place had such a great staff, it ran itself. Still, Enzo hung around a bit now and then, trying to fit in.

Tonight, the place was too loud. Enzo was on edge. After an hour of flashing lights, loud music, and dancing bodies, Enzo headed out. He could be lonely at home. At least it was quiet there. As he stepped outside and the noise died away, Enzo tilted his chin toward the sky and inhaled. It was chilly tonight. He welcomed the cool air after the stifling heat inside. Maybe he was getting old. It sure as hell felt like it.

"What's a sexy guy like you doing out here all alone?"

Enzo turned his head at the question. A college age guy hovered over a sprite of a man, leering.

The curly-haired sprite pulled a sucker from his mouth and tried to be polite. "I'm just waiting on my Uber."

Enzo found himself moving closer as the obviously impaired guy invaded the sprite's personal space. The creepy guy ran his hand down the tiny dude's back, even going as far as to caress the poor guy's ass. "I'll give you a ride. I'll even give you something else to put in your mouth when you finish that sucker."

The sprite jumped away.

Sleazy guy wasn't having it. He moved even closer.

"Nope." The word burst from Enzo before his brain realized what he had done. Enzo couldn't stand by and do nothing. As the oldest of four siblings and a veteran, he was protective by nature. This was his club. He wouldn't let this happen in his parking lot. "Hands off, buddy. We don't touch people without their permission."

Both men turned Enzo's way.

The sleazy guy smirked. "Stay out of this. He wants it."

Enzo looked the sprite's way. The most beautiful eyes he had ever seen stared back at him. They were amber, and he swore they captured the light, reflecting it back at him. A sense of déjà vu washed over him. He swore they had met before. "Do you want this guy touching you?"

The sprite smirked. "Ah, Enzo. Still the hero, I see. I made the mistake of falling for this ruse once. It's been six years. Are you really still playing this game? How much did you pay this guy?"

Enzo was struck dumb. He didn't know which revelation or accusation to address first.

When he didn't speak, the gorgeous gaze slid the sleaze ball's way. "How much is he paying you?"

The guy looked between Enzo and the sprite. He walked away, as if this was too much drama even for human slime.

Enzo watched him go. When he turned back toward the sexy gaze, he found amber eyes watching him expectantly. "Have we met?"

The snort that met his question was epic. "It's a sad fucking day when you've played so many men the same way you can't remember their names. I'm Aric, if that helps jog your memory at all. No doubt all the names run together by now, though."

The name bounced from the walls of Enzo's brain. A drunken memory rose to the surface. Beautiful eyes. A sexy smirk. "Holy shit. You're the Halloween ballerina. The one that guy cornered at that one party."

Aric rolled his eyes and peered down the street, as if silently begging his Uber to appear. "I love the way you act like you didn't bribe that guy to corner me so you could race to the rescue. Don't you have some women to seduce? I distinctly recall you telling me you had never been with a man before."

Had he said that? Fuck. Enzo had been so deep in a bottle that night, he didn't remember much. It was possible, though. He had made out with a lot of strangers at parties and never went home with men. "It doesn't look like your ride is coming. Let me take you home."

"Pass."

Damn. Enzo wasn't used to being disliked. Everyone liked him. "I'm sorry for whatever I did or said that night. It's no excuse, but I had a lot to drink. I only remember a white tutu and you were wearing a crown. You stunned me." Aric still wouldn't look his way again. Enzo couldn't give up. "Please let me take you home so you can berate me properly while filling in the missing details."

Aric pulled out his phone. He cursed under his breath. Aric plucked the sucker from his mouth and cast another longing look down the street.

He spared Enzo a quick glance. "My Uber cancelled the ride, so I guess I don't have much of a choice. Just so you know, I'm only going with you because I already lived through one night with you without ending up dead in a ditch, but I have pepper spray. I'll use it." He popped the sucker back in his mouth at the promise.

A smile snapped to Enzo's lips. "You should've sprayed the other guy, then."

"The breeze was against me. I would've ended up the one in tears."

Enzo chuckled as he led Aric to his Yukon. He unlocked the doors and opened the passenger side door for Aric. Aric eyed him with more than a hint of suspicion as he climbed inside the SUV. A shot of satisfaction sideswiped Enzo as he closed Aric inside. He had Aric now. Enzo could keep him. Even Enzo was horrified by his thoughts. Aric obviously hated him. Enzo wouldn't be keeping anyone. But he would find out what he had done that Halloween night. He wanted to think he wouldn't tell a stranger that he had never been with a man before—like he was some sort of experiment. The thing was, though, Enzo hadn't actually been with a man. He didn't know how else Aric would know that. It hadn't been until about two years ago, right before he turned thirty, that Enzo fully accepted his bisexuality and that he leaned more toward men. It should have been easier to accept himself, considering his youngest brother was gay and his family fully accepted him. Not to mention, Marco had chased women and men alongside Enzo for years.

Mostly, Enzo had thought he would settle down and have kids someday. He hadn't seen himself settling down with another man. He just hadn't.

Now, as Enzo climbed behind the wheel of his SUV, he wondered why he had been dumb enough to let Aric get away if he had confessed that about himself to Aric six years ago. Damn. Aric was fucking gorgeous. A smile pulled at Enzo's lips as he looked Aric's way, only to find Aric staring back at him with disgust. He fought a laugh. Apparently, he had left a lasting impression in his drunken state. Enzo would have to see what he could do to change that. Suddenly, Enzo didn't feel quite so alone and bored with life. He liked a challenge. Enzo got the feeling he had just met his biggest one yet.

·♥·♥·♥·♥·♥·

Enzo fucking De Luca. Of all the men in the world to trip over again, it had to be him. It wasn't just that they had fucked. Aric had had other one-night stands over the years. This one had been different. Enzo had been like a white knight riding to his rescue. Funnily enough, he had been wearing a knight costume at the time. That should have been Aric's first clue it was a ruse. Enzo had been sexy and sweet. He had fucked Aric like he meant it and whispered silly promises Aric should have seen through immediately. Halfway through the night, everything changed. Aric didn't like to think about that night. His entire life had been ruined. About a year later, Aric ran across the guy Enzo had saved him from. After some talking, it turned out Enzo had paid the guy to get handsy so he could race in to help. Aric had been everyone's fool that night. It had cost him everything. Never again.

"I need your address."

Aric plucked the sucker from his mouth and rattled off his address. He wrapped his lips around the cherry-flavored candy again and rode in silence. Aric fought the urge to chomp into the sucker, taking his frustrations out on its hard shell. Enzo smelled good. That wasn't fair. He was also just as tall as Aric remembered. Bastard.

"Were you at The Aviator tonight? I didn't see you there."

"I agreed to a ride. Not conversation." Aric hated he felt guilty for being an asshole when he was the wronged party. He should revel in ripping out Enzo's soul. That just wasn't Aric. He wasn't cruel. Bitter, yes, but not mean.

Enzo didn't respond, as if honoring Aric's wishes.

Aric sighed. Sometimes, it sucked being a nice person. "I was down the street at Pizzazz Pizza Parlor and Arcade. It was my niece's birthday party. Afterward, I walked down to the club and thought about going inside. I decided I'd rather go home." The thought of family reminded Aric of something. "Where's your twin? I thought you two were sewn together at the hip."

Enzo kept his gaze locked on the road. "He's on a naval carrier in the middle of the Pacific. I got out a year ago. He stayed in."

Aric saw the way Enzo's grip tightened on the steering wheel and the muscle that twitched in Enzo's jaw. He had hit a nerve. Aric didn't want to soften, but he also didn't like silence. "Are you back in L.A. or just visiting again?" He fully expected every word Enzo spoke to be a lie, but he still wanted to hear Enzo's answer.

"I'm back. My youngest brother, Tito, got married last year. I wanted to be closer to him and back in my hometown."

They had only spent one night together. Aric didn't know much about the guy. A hint of animosity melted away. It was possible he shouldn't be so angry. They had both been drunk that night. It wasn't like Enzo was the only one-night stand Aric ever had. He likely should let go of all his animosity. It was a long time ago. Enzo had made him feel special that night. It was stupid. Aric didn't feel important very often. That didn't mean he couldn't try to bridge the gap. After all, Enzo was taking him home. He could make small talk for ten minutes.

"What does Tito do for a living?"

Enzo hesitated—like he didn't want to say. When he answered, he sounded exactly like he knew Aric wouldn't believe him. "He's Hudson Vincent's personal bodyguard."

The thing was, Aric only knew Enzo as a liar. If Enzo had picked any other artist, Aric would have immediately fallen out laughing at Enzo's audacity. In this case, though, Aric was likely Hudson Vincent's biggest fan. He practically stalked the guy's every move online. Aric knew exactly who Hudson's bodyguard was and who he had married. An image of Tito De Luca came to mind. The last names matched. They had the same eyes. Fuck his life. Enzo really was related to Hudson Vincent's bodyguard.

Aric took a calming breath. He would not ask any questions. Enzo had fucked him over the last time they had been together. Aric couldn't let Enzo think he had a shot at screwing him again.

"That sounds like a busy job." Aric wanted to pat himself on the back for sounding so calm.

Enzo visibly relaxed. He flashed Aric a smile. "Not so much anymore. With Hudson retired, Tito is enjoying the quiet life."

A sardonic laugh escaped Aric. "If I didn't hate you, I'd say you have to introduce me sometime."

Enzo cast him a quick glance. He looked confused. "Hate seems a bit extreme."

Aric turned to stare out his window. They were almost at his apartment. "But it isn't," he muttered more for himself.

"You still haven't told me what I did."

Bitterness tugged at the corners of Aric's mouth, turning his smile caustic. "It doesn't matter."

"It obviously does."

The only thing obvious to Aric was Enzo's inability to leave things alone. Enzo pulled into a parking space outside Aric's apartment. Aric grabbed the door handle. "No. Genuinely. It doesn't matter. You gave me a ride home. I doubt we'll ever set eyes on each other again. Have a nice life, Sir Enzo." Aric slipped from the SUV and headed inside as fast as his feet would take him without running. He thought he had dealt with Enzo's betrayal. Now Aric realized he was still hurt. It didn't matter that it was ridiculous for him to feel anything at all. Aric had thought he was special. If life had taught him anything, it was that the opposite was true.

·♥·♥·♥·♥·♥·

For ten minutes, Enzo sat outside Aric's apartment in a stunned silence. Aric calling him Sir Enzo stirred to life a memory. Red lipstick. Aric whispering for him to go slow. Enzo blinked several times. It couldn't be true. Enzo had never actually had sex with a man. He had done a lot of flirting and had some heavy make-out sessions. But Enzo hadn't been brave enough to cross that line yet. Right? Fuck. He had been really drunk that Halloween, but surely he would remember having sex with another man for the first time in his life.

He cast a desperate look around. This place looked familiar too. Hadn't that party been in one of these apartments? Not Aric's, but a few doors down. Another memory flashed through Enzo's mind. They had held hands while walking from the apartment where the party was held to Aric's. Enzo had pinned Aric against the door.

"I don't know what I'm doing."

"Don't worry. I do."

Fuck. Aric was right. Enzo was a terrible person. He remembered. Not everything, but enough. Enzo's cock stirred despite his guilt. Aric had been beautiful. Amazing. Enzo had been a nervous and drunken mess. He didn't remember leaving. Enzo had woken up at Tito's house the next day. Hudson's personal driver had picked up Marco and him from the party. At least, that was what Marco had said. Enzo had forgotten all about Aric. He couldn't believe he was so stupid. Aric should have spit in his face. He would find a way to make it up to Aric. Enzo had money now. He had connections. Enzo could make some calls and learn everything about Aric. Aric didn't stand a chance.

First, Enzo needed Aric to know he could count on Enzo if he needed anything. Enzo dug through the contents of his glove box and console. He found an old flyer for a car wash and a pen. After scratching out another quick apology, Enzo wrote his number at the bottom. Likely, Aric wouldn't call no matter what. That was fine. Enzo just needed to know Aric had his number. He jogged to the door and slipped the paper into the crack. Soon enough, Aric would realize how persistent Enzo could be. Enzo didn't intend to let Aric get away twice. He might be dumb, but he wasn't stupid. Next time, Enzo wouldn't forget a thing.

Chapter Two

♥

WILSON & COX LAW Firm sat tucked away in a high-class area in West Hollywood. The entire building looked to be made of glass and gleamed in the sunshine. Even though there were only two lawyers named on the door, Wilson & Cox had over three hundred employees on the payroll. They were professional, efficient, and ruthless. That was only a few of the reasons Enzo had chosen them to handle all his legal affairs. The biggest deciding factor had been Baker Cox. He was the Cox in the name. Baker had been Cooper's family lawyer for years. Cooper and Baker had their issues, but Enzo believed Baker had a good heart. That was a rare thing in L.A. attorneys.

Baker was also relentless. Enzo needed that right now.

Inside the law firm, Enzo hopped on the elevator and rode to the top floor of the twenty-five-story building. It was the only floor in the building that was split into just two office spaces. One half went to Joshua Wilson and the other to Baker. They were penthouse-type offices with every luxury a wealthy attorney could need. A lone secretary sat between the two spaces, waiting to delegate any work Joshua or Baker needed. Also, it was her job to ensure no one made it inside either office without an appointment. Luckily, Enzo had one of those.

Sandra glanced up as the elevator door opened and Enzo stepped out.

"Good morning, Mr. De Luca. Mr. Cox is expecting you." She went back to work, dismissing Enzo immediately.

It wasn't like Enzo to not be able to charm someone, but Sandra was one of those people. She never gave Enzo enough of her attention for him to try. Enzo always assumed she was too busy to chat and headed inside Baker's office.

The glass door led into a boardroom that was always empty as far as Enzo could tell. Behind the long wooden table was another door. Enzo headed through that one and into extravagance. The full wall of windows had an amazing view of the hills. Plush white furniture scattered throughout the room. Baker sat in the center of a large couch in the center of the room. He straightened away from the file he was bent over as Enzo came through the door. His brown hair was perfectly styled, and his expensive suit looked tailor made. It likely cost more than Enzo's car. The gray material made the man's steel-colored gaze stand out even more. He smiled as he spotted Enzo.

"Enzo. Is it ten already? I could've sworn I hadn't been here more than an hour."

Enzo smiled at Baker's smooth British accent. He liked listening to Baker talk. "Actually, I'm five minutes late."

Baker stood and motioned for Enzo to join him. "Ah, well. I hadn't noticed. How have you been?"

Enzo sat, and Baker reclaimed his spot while Enzo answered. "I've been good. How about you?"

Baker nodded. "Splendid. Things have been as busy as ever. I was just going over the file from our investigators." He slid the file Enzo's way and Enzo leaned forward to eye the contents as Baker pulled them from the folder. "Aric Long is a twenty-eight-year-old construction worker for Golden Key Contractors. As far as I can tell, he goes to work and comes home. That's it. He doesn't interact with anyone." Baker handed Enzo a couple of photos of Aric. In both shots, Aric wore a hard hat and an orange vest. He stood away from all the other workers outside a construction zone in one of the images. In the another, he sat under a tree alone. Baker pointed at that image. "He eats lunch alone every day.

I'm not sure what you're looking for, but Aric Long seems to be just your everyday loner. He goes to work, stops by a few shops occasionally on his way home. Otherwise, nothing."

Enzo had no intention of admitting this was no more than high-dollar stalking. "Did you find out his contact information?"

Baker nodded and tapped on a typed page inside the folder. "I have everything. His number, address, how much he makes, which is barely enough to survive, by the bye. As far as I can see, he isn't anything special."

Enzo disagreed, but he didn't bother arguing. "Thanks for this." Enzo stacked everything inside the folder and stood. "This is exactly what I needed."

Baker's eyebrows rose. "Exactly what you needed is nothing?"

A smile snapped to Enzo's lips. "This isn't nothing. It's enough to get me started."

Baker's open confusion doubled. "As much as I really wish to pepper you with questions, I'm somewhat afraid of learning something untoward. Then again, this falls under attorney-client privilege. So, what in the hell is going on?"

"I'm righting a wrong."

Baker's expression cleared. "Oh. That's fine, then. You're definitely in the financial position to help someone. This fellow looks as if he could use a hand."

"Sure." Enzo was cool with Baker creating his own story for why Enzo would hire him to find out everything about a stranger. He waved the folder toward Baker. "Thank you for this." A thought struck. "Is the address and time listed in here for when and where Aric eats lunch alone?"

"Of course."

A smile that felt evil even to him stretched Enzo's lips. "Great."

Let the stalking begin.

·❤·❤·❤·❤·❤·

The shade from the oak tree next to the construction site gave Aric a nice respite from the blazing sun. As always, Aric did his best to remove the dirt and germs from his hands with wet wipes before unzipping his lunch box. He was exhausted today. For six weeks, his crew had been on twelve-hour shifts. The extra pay had been nice, but everything hurt. All Aric wanted was a nap.

"Is it okay if I sit with you?"

Aric glanced up. His mind froze at the sight of Enzo hovering over him. "Um."

"I'll take that as a yes." Enzo sat before Aric could argue.

"How did you find me?" Aric hoped the disgust in his voice spoke for itself.

Enzo didn't seem the least bit put off by Aric's tone. "I hired someone to find you."

The eye roll was completely out of Aric's control. "No. Really. How did you find me?"

Enzo shrugged. "I work one block over. What are you having for lunch?"

For some reason Aric couldn't fully explain, he fought a blush at the question. Aric ate the same thing every day, and he ate like a twelve-year-old.

Partially because he was boring, but mostly because he was poor.

While sitting facing him, Enzo opened a brown paper bag. "Don't laugh, but I have one of those crackers and lunch meat kits they make for kids. It has a cookie and juice box inside. They're not so bad."

"That's not enough food for you," Aric said without thought. Enzo was a big guy. A handful of crackers and a single cookie wouldn't sustain him. Aric flipped open his lunch box without meeting Enzo's gaze. "I always pack extras since I never know when they'll make me stay late. It's not very exciting, but I have a peanut butter and jelly sandwich and chips you can have."

"Thank you. That sounds great." Aric passed Enzo a sandwich while Enzo kept talking. "It's been years since I've had a PB and J. I don't know why I stopped eating them. I love them."

Aric didn't know why he didn't demand Enzo leave him in peace. "Do you really work nearby?"

Enzo nodded as he took a bite of his sandwich. He swallowed before responding. "I work at that club where I saw you the other night, The Aviator."

"You left the Navy to work at a bar?" Aric bit into his sandwich while he waited for Enzo to answer.

Enzo shrugged. "I was in for long enough to be eligible for a percentage of my pay for life, and sleep is underrated. For years, I was up before the sun and wishing I could sleep just a few more hours. Truthfully, I've always been a bit of a night owl. Late nights, beer, and sleeping in. A bar seemed a nice change."

Aric shook his head. "You could be an airline pilot with your flight experience." He didn't understand Enzo. It made no sense to go from being a pilot for the Navy to a bartender. That was insane.

Enzo waved off Aric's suggestion. "Pilots are never home. I'm tired. Don't you ever want to toss all responsibility to the wind? Don't you ever want to be someone new?"

For a moment, Aric lost himself in Enzo's hazel eyes. He felt seen. Aric always wanted to be someone else. Unfortunately, he had quit school the moment he could and didn't have many options without a high school diploma. Sometimes reality paralyzed him. Aric had quit school due to relentless bullying, only to step into real life where no one accepted him. "It must be nice to have choices," Aric said after a moment. He finished his sandwich to stop himself from exposing anymore of his soul. Enzo had already proved he would stomp on Aric's feelings at the drop of a hat.

Enzo polished off his sandwich and opened the lunch he had brought for himself. He held it out to Aric, silently offering to share. "If you could do any job you wanted, what would it be? The only limit is your imagination."

A laugh escaped Aric as he stacked a slice of cheese and lunch meat on a cracker. "If imagination is the limit, I'd be someone's sugar baby for sure. I've had some sort of job since I was twelve. It was just my mom and us kids, growing up. I had to help. If I wasn't babysitting my little sister, I was bagging groceries under the table at this little family-owned store down the street from us. I've always done what I have to do. So, if I had a choice, I'd choose nothing."

Enzo held his stare and nodded along —like he got it. "What are—"

"Enzo. Enzo De Luca, is that you?"

Enzo looked away at the interruption. Aric's supervisor Danny moved their way. He was smiling, which was something Aric had never seen. "Damn, boy. It is you."

Enzo stood and brushed off the seat of his pants before shaking Danny's hand. "Hey there, Daniel. How have you been?"

Danny made a dismissive gesture at Enzo's question. "Ah, you know. Just working. I heard you'd moved back to L.A. and opened a nightclub. How's business going?"

"It's going good. Tito's husband backed me, so I had a leg up on that end. I can't take much credit."

Danny scoffed. "Please. Don't forget I served with you. I know you're a damn hard worker. I don't doubt you've earned every bit of success."

Aric stared at his lap and wished the ground would swallow him whole. Of course Enzo owned The Aviator. It was called The Aviator, for fuck's sake. It also figured Enzo would be friends with Aric's boss, because life enjoyed making him the butt of every joke. Aric repacked his lunch box and stood. For a moment, he had felt a hint of kinship with Enzo. Aric should have known better. He didn't know why Enzo had sought him out, but it meant less than nothing. They were nothing alike. Sometimes, Aric wondered if there was anyone out there like him. He felt dumb as hell for all his admissions. Weakness never got him anything.

Aric gathered his things and headed back to the job site. He looped his bag across the opposite shoulder so it was secured across his chest before snapping his safety harness into place. Aric climbed the scaffolding while keeping his mind blank.

"Was that your boyfriend?"

Aric ignored the jibe as he climbed past one of his coworkers.

"Shut the hell up, Gary," Danny yelled, cutting in. "That was one of my old Navy buddies. He doesn't swing that way."

Aric put his earbuds in and blocked out the conversation. No good could come of engaging. It had been nice to have company for lunch, but Aric wasn't sure it was worth the bullying he would take. As angry as Aric was with Enzo for walking away from him, Aric couldn't blame him. The price

Aric paid to be true to himself wasn't anywhere near worth it. He wasn't happy. No one liked him, and he didn't fit in anywhere he went. If Enzo could choose, he was right not to pick Aric. There was nothing worthwhile about his life. Nothing at all.

Chapter Three

♥

WITH THE FIRST STEP in his stalking plan complete, Enzo wasn't sure how things were going. Aric had slipped away while Enzo had been distracted by one of his old Navy acquaintances. Enzo hadn't known how to get Aric's attention again before he left, so he decided to show up at Aric's apartment instead. It was a risk. Likely, Aric would look through the peephole and refuse to answer. He was probably wasting his time, but Enzo had nothing else going on and he liked Aric. Also, Enzo wanted to remember more about their night together. He felt at sea. Aric was the only person to make Enzo feel less alone in months. They had shared something Enzo wanted back. He didn't know how to voice that. Until last night, Enzo thought he hadn't crossed the line into actual sex with another man. Now he knew that wasn't true. Enzo wanted that memory.

Enzo knocked on Aric's door with his heart in his throat. He really didn't want to get turned away. Aric answered, looking half asleep. His hair stood in every direction and one side of his face was red and had lines through it like the impression of a pillow. He blinked at the sight of Enzo.

"Oh. It's you." He turned away, as if he meant to close the door in Enzo's face.

Enzo shoved his foot in the door, stopping it from closing. "Please, Aric. I'm really sorry for every way I've wronged you. You're the only man I've ever been with and I want that night back."

Aric turned and met Enzo's stare. He didn't look softened by Enzo's apology or confession.

Enzo rushed to clarify his words. "I meant, I need to remember that night. Back then, I didn't know what I wanted. I do now and I have this feeling in my gut that we shared something special, but the full memory is just out of sight. Please, just let me spend some time with you so maybe I'll remember."

"I'm really tired, Enzo."

Enzo nodded. Aric sounded and looked exhausted. "I know. I'm not trying to make your life harder. Just give me a chance to prove it."

Aric walked away, leaving the door open. Enzo took it as a silent invitation to stay. He quickly followed Aric inside and closed the door. Enzo tossed a cursory glance around at the room. The place was clean and the furniture dark. Nothing sparked a memory. Aric crossed the room and fell face down across the couch. With a smile, Enzo moved to sit nearby in a recliner. He tried to stay quiet. It was obvious Aric needed to rest. Enzo was a man of his word. He didn't want anything other than Aric's company. If Aric needed sleep, Enzo would stay by his side.

He was so beautiful. Enzo couldn't stop staring at Aric. He had obviously recently showered and fallen asleep with wet hair. Aric wore only a pair of short cotton shorts and a ragged tank top. The tank top rode up when Aric plopped down, showing some bare skin. Enzo's gaze locked on the smooth, pale surface. He fought the urge to kiss the exposed area. Then he spotted the material peeking out above Aric's shorts. A thong. Goddamn. Enzo wanted this man. It was no wonder he had been ensnared years ago.

"You're staring at me."

Enzo bit back a smile. "Go to sleep and you won't know. I'm just inspecting your body, hoping to kick-start my memories."

Aric rolled onto his back and draped his arm across his eyes. "Do you have any idea how insulting it is to be forgotten? You fed me that bullshit story about being the first man you've ever been with, and then waltzed away, forgetting I exist. It's like I was such a common experience, I didn't stick to your brain in any way."

Even though Aric's voice was groggy, Enzo still heard the hurt tinging his words. "Not only were you the first, but you're also the only man I've ever been with. I didn't forget on purpose. It's more like I drank my weight in liquor to work up the courage to leave with you in the first place. I've started remembering bits and pieces since you called me Sir Enzo. I want to remember everything. You're not someone I want to forget."

Aric didn't respond right away. Enzo thought he had fallen asleep. Finally, Aric made a humming noise—like he understood. "I'll help you, but you have to let me sleep first. So tired right now."

"Get some rest. I'll be here when you wake up."

"That's what you said last time right before you fell asleep. I didn't see you again for six years."

That wouldn't happen again. Enzo needed to know why it happened last time. He wasn't leaving until he knew everything. Something didn't set right with him about that night. Enzo had to fix it. He couldn't live with Aric's hatred. Enzo could live with a lot, but not that. He would make this right, somehow.

· ♥ · ♥ · ♥ · ♥ · ♥ ·

Everything hurt. Aric hadn't meant to sleep the entire night on the couch. His eyes had been too heavy. Aric meant to rest them. The next thing he knew, the alarm went off in his bedroom and Aric scrambled to shut it down before it woke the man sleeping in his recliner. Enzo had stayed. He looked uncomfortable as fuck. Aric draped a blanket over him and got ready for work. He would leave a note for Enzo to lock up when he left. Aric had nothing to steal. It didn't matter if Enzo stayed.

After running through his morning routine, making his lunch, and pouring some coffee in a thermos, Aric spent a few minutes watching Enzo sleep. His hair was shaggier than it had been when they first met. Aric assumed that was due to him no longer being in the military. A slight rebellion or act of personal freedom, perhaps. No matter the reason, Aric liked it. Enzo didn't look as severe. Aric's gaze dropped to Enzo's lips. They were full yet firm. He had kissed Aric with the surety of a man who had kissed a thousand people. Aric remembered everything about that night. No one had ever made him feel so much in such a short time. In only a few hours, Enzo had filled him with such hope for the future. Maybe that was the part Aric didn't know how to forgive. He could have lived with a one-night stand with zero promises.

The slightest hint of hope always ripped Aric's heart out. No one understood what it was like to be him. He was the outcast.

Shaking off his maudlin, Aric found his spare key so Enzo could lock the deadbolt behind him. He scratched out a quick note explaining where he had gone and how to lock the door. Aric would have to trust him to leave the key under the mat. There was no other way to lock up his place. With his note written and the key left behind, Aric headed out to work. If he didn't make it to the bus stop in time, he would be late for work. Aric couldn't risk that. He already wasn't liked. Aric couldn't give them a single reason to give him the boot. He didn't know how to do anything else.

The morning passed the way it always did. Aric kept his earbuds in, and no one tried talking to him. He did his job efficiently, the way he did every day. Lunch time hit and everyone split into their friendship groups. Aric climbed down the scaffolding and headed for his spot in the shade. Alone. Except halfway to the tree, he spotted Enzo waiting for him. He smiled at the sight of Aric, as if seeing Aric made his day. Something shifted in Aric's chest. No one lit at the sight of him. It was nice. Aric joined Enzo under the tree.

"Hey. I figured you'd still be asleep. Isn't nightclub ownership exhausting?"

Enzo winced. "I guess I should've mentioned I was the owner."

Aric sat. "Nah. You don't owe me anything. Keep your secrets."

"It's not a secret," Enzo said with a shrug. "I guess I just don't feel like I earned it. Today, I grabbed a box of Uncrustables from the store."

A smile snapped to Aric's lips. "Seriously? I haven't had one of those in years."

Enzo pulled the box from the bag. "We can share them. There's like four in the box."

Aric eyed the box. "Nope. That's the big box. There's ten in that one. Oooh, you got the grape jelly ones. Those are the best. Did you know they have some chocolate hazelnut ones too? You can put them in an air fryer and then put powdered sugar on them while they're hot. It's like a carnival treat."

"We should do that one night," Enzo said as he tore into the box. "I've never used an air fryer, but I'm sure I could figure it out."

Aric accepted the sandwich from Enzo. "I only have one because my sister bought me one last year for Christmas. She wanted me to have one at my house. That way, when Grace spends the night, I can cook her chicken nuggets the way she likes them. That's all she'll eat, pizza and chicken nuggets. Three meals a day."

"Is Grace your niece?"

Aric nodded as he chewed.

Enzo let him eat. "I have twin nephews. Ethan and Aiden. They're five. I never get to see them, though. They live in Mississippi."

"That must be hard."

Enzo shrugged. "When you're always alone, it's amazing how other people start to feel unreal to you. Like I know I have family, but it's almost like I don't anymore. Tito and Cooper are the only ones I see."

Aric's heart twisted. He completely understood. Not only with his family, but with everyone. It was like he lived in a computer simulation. No one else felt real because he was so disconnected from everyone. He had to think of it that way. Otherwise, the loneliness would drown him. "I would think a nightclub owner would never be alone."

Enzo flashed him a sexy smile that made Aric's stomach flutter. "Even my business doesn't need me. Like I said, I didn't earn it. I'd planned to open a small bar with Marco and our friend Jake. They backed out last minute and decided to stay in the Navy. Honestly, I should've seen it coming. Marco has won heroism awards and shit. It's his life. He wants to be a full career Navy man. But their decision left me fucked." Aric heard the hurt in Enzo's voice. He held on to every word. Enzo made a helpless gesture. "Then Cooper stepped in. He comes from money and his lawyers are the best. They have a huge staff with all sorts of business skills. They decided a nightclub would do better in L.A. than a small everyone-knows-your-name bar. Cooper invested the money. The place blew everyone's expectations out of the water. So now I'm just sort of adrift. My club runs itself. All my friends are back in San Diego and my family is scattered across the world. Marco is currently deployed." Enzo shrugged and took a bite of his sandwich, as if embarrassed by admitting so much.

Aric couldn't let Enzo feel exposed. "I've worked here for ten years. They hired me right after I dropped out of high school. I'm still in the same position I was ten years ago. They won't move me up the ladder because they think I'm odd. That's okay. I am, but it never gets easier here. You think you'd get used to no one ever talking to you unless they're insulting you, but I don't. I just keep my earbuds in and the music going all day, blocking them out. Then I go home, eat, sleep, and get up to do it all over again. All the friends I had when I was younger have moved on. They're married or happily cohabitating in the suburbs. It's just me now." Aric opened his water and took a drink to keep from looking directly at Enzo after exposing his heart. He told himself Enzo couldn't hurt him worse than he already had, so what did a little more exposure matter. Still, Aric didn't like anyone seeing him as weak.

"I was in the Navy with Danny. I'm not surprised he runs a crew of intolerant bullies. He obviously keeps you around for a reason, though. I'm guessing you're a damn hard worker."

He was. Not that it mattered. "Speaking of being a hard worker, I guess I should get back to work. I can't give them a reason to treat me worse."

Enzo's gaze moved over Aric's face, as if looking for something only he knew. "Okay. I'll see you later."

Aric gathered his things while trying hard not to hope. He didn't even like Enzo. Right? Aric wasn't an idiot. He knew he was lying to himself. Aric just couldn't let himself get invested. Maybe he would see Enzo. Maybe he wouldn't. Only time would tell if Enzo was only passing the time until he found a new group of friends. Danny headed Enzo's way. Aric put his earbuds in and didn't look back. Enzo would move on with people on his level. Aric didn't doubt that for a moment. It was best he didn't think otherwise. He was no one. Enzo would realize it eventually.

·❤·❤·❤·❤·❤·

Enzo hadn't cared for Danny back when they had served together. He didn't understand why the guy kept interrupting Enzo's time with Aric—like they were old friends. Enzo knew Aric had to work and Enzo couldn't get him in trouble or draw too much attention Aric's way. He didn't wait around to see if Aric got anymore breaks throughout the day. Instead, he headed back to the store.

After picking up some of the chocolate hazelnut Uncrustables, Enzo grabbed a couple of steaks and sides. He couldn't make Aric's job any easier, but he could make Aric dinner. Enzo doubted Aric would let him keep the key to Aric's apartment. He needed to take advantage of the situation while he could.

One trip to the grocery store for dinner led to two after Enzo realized Aric had next to no food in his house. Enzo didn't know what Aric liked, but he grabbed a little of everything. It took him a couple of hours, but Aric's refrigerator, freezer, and pantry were all stocked. Even though it was a lot for one person, Enzo hoped to be invited back and he had bought a lot of things that would last for a while. Everything about Aric's life pissed Enzo off. Aric needed someone to take care of him.

Enzo worked the entire day to make Aric's life easier, buying things, cleaning, and cooking. By the time Aric walked through the door, he looked resigned to the fact Enzo was still there.

"I thought you'd be gone by now."

Aric's tone didn't give any hints to his feelings on the matter. Enzo wrapped himself in his overabundance of confidence and ran with it. "You told me you would help me remember something, but you slept all night. I thought we could try again tonight."

Aric tossed his keys and phone on the table by the door. "Well, something smells good."

Still, his tone gave nothing away. "I figured you'd be hungry."

With a wary glance toward the kitchen, Aric headed that way. He set his lunchbox on the counter. His hand hovered over it as his gaze moved the fresh bread and unopened bags of chips on the counter.

Enzo jumped in. "I hope you don't mind, but I picked up some groceries for you too. After I grabbed us some steaks and baked potatoes for tonight, I noticed you didn't really have any seasonings. One purchase led to another, and I bought too much stuff."

Aric eyed the fridge like he was scared to find out how much was too much. "Yeah. I don't have a car and it's kind of a pain to transport groceries on the bus. I only buy a few things at a time."

Fuck. Everything Enzo learned about Aric made things a little worse. He couldn't imagine trying to ride the bus everywhere through this part of town.

"Well, now you shouldn't need anything for a while."

Aric's gaze moved around the kitchen as if he didn't want to meet Enzo's stare. "Oh. Thank you, I guess. How much do I owe you?"

Enzo fought a growl. "You don't owe me anything. I plan to stick around until I get the memory I came for. The least I can do is stock your fridge and make you dinner. I know you don't want me around."

Aric's gaze snapped to Enzo's at Enzo's claim. "I want you around."

The muscles in Enzo's stomach clenched. His knees weakened. Aric had the most beautiful eyes and the softest-looking lips. Enzo remembered approaching him that Halloween. He hadn't been able to stop himself. Aric was like a siren.

Aric's gaze slid away, as if embarrassed by his confession. He moved to the stove and inspected their food.

Enzo jumped at the chance to change the subject. "I didn't know what time you got home, so I've been keeping everything warm."

"It looks delicious." He turned back Enzo's way. "Is it okay if I take a shower before we eat?"

"Yeah. I'm in no hurry."

With a nod, Aric slipped past Enzo and headed for his bedroom. Enzo knew from spending all day in the one-bedroom apartment and snooping, the only bathroom was inside the bedroom. It was a small apartment. There was a tiny living room with only a couch, recliner, coffee table, and entertainment center. The kitchen was minuscule. Only the half wall separating the kitchen from the living room—that also doubled as a bar—kept the kitchen from feeling claustrophobic. Aric's bedroom was the same size as the living room. The only furniture inside that room was a bed and a dresser. Oddly, Aric's bathroom was the nicest room in the apartment. It had a built-in vanity with lots of surrounding lights. There was a walk-in shower with a separate tub. Double sinks. For such a small place, the bathroom was surprising. The bedroom also had a big walk-in closet. Enzo had already snooped. In his defense, he had hoped he would recall some details about their night together by checking out the bedroom. He hadn't.

When Enzo reappeared, he wore the same basic outfit as he had worn last night. Enzo's curiosity was through the roof. He eyed Aric's ass as Aric headed for the kitchen. He wondered if another thong hid behind Aric's short shorts.

Side by side, they made their plates. Aric opened the fridge and froze. He eyed the contents before opening the freezer to do the same. From there, he moved to the pantry.

"Holy shit."

"I might've gotten carried away." Even Enzo heard the guilt in his voice.

Aric's gaze moved his way. He looked shell-shocked. "Are you planning to move in?"

A smile snapped to Enzo's lips. "No, but I eat a lot and I'm intruding on your time. The least I can do is pull my weight."

Aric moved back to the fridge and grabbed two sodas. He set the drinks on the bar between the kitchen and living room. There was exactly enough room for two barstools. Two people. They carried their plates to the other side and sat. Side by side, they ate in silence. It wasn't uncomfortable. They made some small talk between bites. Nothing heavy. Aric complimented his cooking. Enzo asked about his day. After they ate, they washed dishes together. Aric washed. Enzo dried. It was nice. The tiny kitchen felt cozy. For the first time in a long time, Enzo felt at peace.

As they headed back to living room, Aric stopped at the bar. "I was thinking, maybe we should try walking through that night, step by step. Kind of like a reenactment. That might jog your memories."

A chuckle that sounded evil even to Enzo slipped from his lips. "Go put on the tutu. I'm game."

Aric rolled his eyes. "I don't have that outfit anymore. That was six years ago. I'm not anywhere near the size I was at twenty-two."

That sounded like bullshit to Enzo, but whatever. Aric hadn't punched him for the suggestion, so there was that. Enzo's unharmed state made him brave. "Do you have anything like it?"

Aric didn't as much as blink. "Yes, but I don't see how that matters."

A wicked smile tugged at Enzo's lips. "It might help me remember the exact moment I looked your way." Enzo already recalled that moment. Aric had looked lonely and beautiful—like a lost angel.

Aric nodded. "That's actually a good idea. Give me a second." He rushed to the bedroom. Enzo's gaze followed. Aric didn't bother shutting the door, probably out of habit. Enzo couldn't force his stare away from Aric as he grabbed an outfit from the closet and stripped. Goddamn. He wore another thong. It was lace. Enzo reached down and adjusted his cock when it stirred. He realized there was no hope for him when Aric slipped on a short dress. It was like an all-white maid's outfit.

Enzo headed for the couch and sat. He tried to hide his erection as Aric headed back to the living room.

"Okay. Let's start from the beginning." He moved to stand next to the bar. "This apartment isn't that much different from the one we were in. It's just smaller. Now, I was standing here, trying not to get crushed by the crowd when Grant approached."

"Who's Grant?"

A line appeared between Aric's eyebrows. "The guy you paid to accost me."

Irritation ran through Enzo. "I absolutely did not do that."

Aric made a dismissive gesture. "It doesn't matter. I was standing here—"

"It absolutely matters," Enzo said, interrupting Aric. "I didn't pay anyone. Why do you think that?"

A loud sigh burst from Aric. "Because I ran into Grant about a year later and he apologized. He said you'd paid him to accost me so you could rescue me. Also, to bring me a roofied drink, but whatever."

Enzo shot to his feet. "Are you fucking kidding me? I don't even know anyone named Grant."

Aric held his stare. For a moment, he didn't speak. Finally, he shook his head and motioned Enzo closer. "It doesn't matter. Come here."

Enzo moved to stand where Aric wanted him, but he didn't let it go. "It matters. Say you believe me."

A small smile touched Aric's lips, and he chuckled. "Stop. We're doing our reenactment. This won't work if you can't let go of that one detail. You've just shoved Grant away from me."

Even though Enzo was beyond frustrated, he played along. He stared down at Aric, going through the motions of that night. "I remember this part. You thanked me and it was like everyone else disappeared. For a moment, we just stared at each other in silence."

Aric visibly swallowed as he stared back at Enzo. "I remember. It was like sparks or a connection. I don't know how to explain it."

Enzo nodded. "Yes. Exactly. I couldn't look away from you. Then some guy shoved a drink between us, and you looked his way, breaking the spell."

Aric nodded. "That was Grant again. He handed me a drink and said, 'Truce.' He claims that was part of your plan too. A second rescue. You took the drink from me and chastised me for accepting a drink from a stranger. I thought I had met a genuinely nice guy."

As frustrated as Enzo was with Aric's lack of faith in him, Enzo couldn't shake the magic of the moment either. Aric had been right to suggest going through the motions of that night. He recalled exactly how he felt in that first few minutes of meeting Aric. Enzo had known right then exactly what he wanted in life. He wanted Aric. Enzo took a sip of the drink he had left on the bar.

Aric's expression changed as he followed the motion. He looked horrified. "Holy shit."

Enzo froze. "What?"

Aric took the can from Enzo and set it on the bar. "That's exactly what happened that night. You took the drink from me and we spent a few minutes flirting. Then you took a sip from the cup. I swiped it from you and set it aside, reminding you you'd just fussed at me, warning me not you drink it. You drugged yourself. It was just a little." Aric practically danced in place with horror. As Enzo looked on, Aric got more upset by the second as he spoke. "You likely wouldn't have felt the effects right away. That explains everything, though. That's why you don't remember." Aric pressed his hand to his stomach. "Oh, shit. That's why you passed out and wouldn't wake up when your brother showed up here, banging on the door."

"Marco showed up here?"

Aric nodded and started pacing. "He said I'd tricked you and drugged you. That you never would've left that party with me otherwise. He had some guys help him carry you out. The whole time, he screamed I was a rapist, and he should call the cops, but he wouldn't embarrass you like that. All my friends stopped talking to me because Marco told them I'd drugged you. Fuck." Aric was pale as a ghost.

Enzo was furious. "What?"

Aric kept pacing. He looked like he might be sick. "Shit. He was right. You drank that roofied drink. I wanted you so badly that I didn't even think about it, but your brother was right." Aric stopped pacing. There were tears in his eyes. "You never would've wanted me if not for that drink."

Enzo closed the distance between them and claimed Aric's mouth. Aric jerked back as if Enzo had slapped him. Enzo wasn't having it. He snagged the back of Aric's head and hauled him in for a kiss. Enzo held Aric in place while he toyed with Aric's lips. Finally, Aric's muscles relaxed in Enzo's hold. His lips parted. Enzo attacked. He swiped his tongue across Aric's, twisting and teasing. Enzo wanted to kick Marco's ass. He wanted to touch Aric even more. Enzo felt like he had been missing part of himself for years. Now he knew why. It was Aric.

·♥·♥·♥·♥·♥·

Aric's heart raced and he could barely breathe. He didn't know if it was from lust or pain. All these years, he had been so angry. He had lost all his friends after that party. Everyone thought he had tricked and drugged Enzo. A pain sliced through his chest. Aric pushed Enzo away.

"I'm sorry. I can't." Aric blindly headed for the bedroom. He stripped off his dress as he went. There was a reason he rarely dressed like this any longer.

He couldn't be the person he wanted to be. Everyone thought he'd tricked a straight man into sex. Aric had been living with the rage of that for years. Now it was true, and Aric couldn't think. He couldn't breathe. Aric had done the one thing he couldn't live with.

With the dress gone, Aric sat on the end of the bed and tried to catch his breath. He hadn't been himself since that night. Aric had known something wasn't right. Enzo had been a little too drunk. Aric had questioned himself a lot over the past six years. He had wondered if he had taken advantage of the situation. When Grant had said Enzo had paid him, Aric had clung to that excuse like a lifeline. Those words had absolved Aric of a majority of his guilt, but—in his heart—Aric had known the truth. He covered his mouth, hoping he didn't lose his dinner. Tears ran down Aric's face unchecked. That night had ruined Aric's life. It turned out he deserved it.

A shirt worked its way over Aric's head. Aric sat still while Enzo dressed him like he would a child. "I can't believe I'm covering this amazing body." Enzo whimpered as he helped Aric with his shorts. "For fuck's sake, that lace thong. Jesus. You're beautiful."

Aric covered his face, torn between embarrassment and tears. Once he was fully dressed, Enzo tumbled him onto the bed and followed him down. He held Aric and spoke quietly against Aric's ear.

"You know I wanted you." Enzo ran his hand down Aric's body, stroking his side. "I crossed that room and flirted with you before I took that drink. You know it. I'm a big guy. One sip of a laced drink won't make me do anything I don't want to do. You felt that spark between us. I know you did."

The tightness in Aric's chest eased. He could still see the way Enzo looked at him that night. Their encounter hadn't been one-sided. Aric drew a ragged breath. "If you didn't pay Grant, and you hadn't been there that night..." He couldn't finish that statement. There was so much horror Enzo didn't know about. That night had started a domino effect that had destroyed him.

"I don't know this Grant guy, but if I ever see him, he'll regret everything about that night." Enzo leaned away and wiped the tears from Aric's face. He looked so kind, Aric couldn't look away. Enzo traced Aric's lips. "I like you."

"I like you too."

At Aric's confession, a small smile touched Enzo's lips. "I remembered something else about that night. You agreed to be mine."

A pain slashed at Aric's heart. That was true. Aric had agreed to be Enzo's. He had never flown higher than he had that night. For the first time in his life, the future had looked bright.

Enzo kissed the corner of Aric's mouth, as if enticing him. "You agreed to be mine even though I lived two hours away."

A watery chuckle escaped Aric. "I was pretty invested after just one night."

"Will you be mine with me living in the same town?"

Aric's mind blanked. He didn't respond.

Enzo didn't look as confident. "I mean, I know I fucked up your life and everything, but I still feel the same. I still want this."

"You didn't fuck up my life. Life just fucked up."

A small smile touched Enzo's lips. "Does that mean you'll give me a shot?"

Aric's heart was so dumb. "I think I have to."

Enzo pulled a face. "You don't have to do anything."

"Yes, I do," Aric argued. "If I don't, I'll always hate myself for missing you."

A bright smile lit Enzo's face. "You won't regret it."

Aric doubted that, but he didn't argue.

Enzo glanced around the room. His gaze landed on the clock. "You have another long day tomorrow. We should go to bed now so I can snuggle you."

"We?"

Enzo nodded, looking serious. "If you're mine, that means cuddles."

Despite everything, Aric couldn't stop smiling. "Okay." He had a terrible feeling this night would haunt him for the rest of his life, but Aric got ready for bed. Aric already had more things to regret than he had hours in the day. He may as well grab some happy memories while he was at it. Tomorrow would come soon enough.

Chapter Four

♥

A MONTH PASSED IN a blur of unexpected happiness. Enzo joined him for lunch every day and slept with Aric every night. They hadn't done anything beyond kissing and cuddling. While Aric was happier than he had ever been, doubts had begun creeping in. Enzo claimed Aric was the only man he had ever been with. The one time they had been together, Enzo had been extremely drunk. It was possible Enzo wasn't as into men as he thought. Honestly, Aric didn't know what to think. He had never had anyone show him so much respect. It was a little too much in his experience. Aric worried Enzo didn't truly want him.

Danny motioned for Aric to take out his earbuds.

Aric only took out one so he could get back to ignoring his boss as quickly as possible.

Once Danny had Aric's attention, he jumped in with both feet. "Why has Enzo been eating lunch with you every day? Are you friends with his little brother or something?"

Aric's face screwed up in confusion. "Tito? No. I've never met the guy."

"Why then?" Danny asked, pressing the subject.

For the first time in his life, Aric didn't want to be honest. He had stuck to the shadows for the past few years. For the most part, everyone left him alone. He didn't want to say anything to stir up bullshit. Aric shrugged. "We're friends and he works down the road from here."

"Huh?"

Aric stood there, wondering if he could put his earbud back in while Danny eyeballed him. Danny wasn't that much taller than Aric, but he was twice as wide and balding. What was left of his brown hair stuck out in every direction. His dark brown gaze moved over Aric's face, making Aric profusely uncomfortable.

After a moment, Danny shrugged. "I guess you two are pretty close in age." With that assessment, Danny walked away, leaving Aric confused. Before Aric could go back to enjoying his music, another of his co-workers moved closer.

"What do you listen to all day, anyhow?"

Aric looked his way. People came and went on construction crews. Aric couldn't say he even knew the guy's name. Every new person they got always fell in with the crowd that hated him and never spoke to Aric. Even though Aric was confused as fuck, he didn't want to be a dick.

"Um, today it's Exile."

A bright smile lit the guy's face. "That's cool. I love those guys. It's a shame they died so young."

Aric nodded. "I would've loved to have seen them in concert just once before they died." They went back to work and Aric put his earbud back in. It had been an odd day. He couldn't wait to tell Enzo about it. Aric froze at the thought. They had only been together a month. Aric shouldn't be this attached. The problem was Enzo was there every night. They slept together and woke up together. Aric had never had that before. He wanted to protect his heart, but he didn't know how. Enzo was everywhere. Maybe it was too late not to get hurt. Aric was sure he would find out soon enough.

·♥·♥·♥·♥·♥·

Since it was Friday night, Enzo likely needed to visit his club. He would see how Aric felt when he got off work. As usual, Enzo waited outside the construction area for Aric's shift to end. He wished Aric would let Enzo buy him a car, but he knew without asking how that would fly. Since Enzo enjoyed doing things for Aric, he settled for driving Aric back and forth to work... for now.

The moment Aric stepped outside the chain-link fence surrounding the worksite, Enzo's entire soul lit. He felt the fire ignite inside him. Enzo realized in that moment he had never known true happiness. He had known joy and had fun. This was different. Being in Aric's company was exactly what Enzo had been waiting for his entire life. He felt a ridiculous smile stretching his lips. It was out of his control.

"Hey."

At Aric's breathless-sounding greeting, an overwhelming need to know if Aric felt the same overcame Enzo. He opened his mouth to ask. "Hey back." Enzo shook his head at his own inability to move forward.

Aric climbed inside. "How was your day?"

As Aric put on his seatbelt, Enzo fought an inner battle against answering the question and still wanting to know if Aric felt as much as Enzo did. "Are you in love with me yet good?"

A loud laugh burst from Aric at the rapid jumble of words that poured from Enzo. "What was that?"

Enzo took a breath and put the SUV in drive. "Sorry. My day was good. I wish I could kiss you, but I don't want to embarrass you at work." Enzo pulled away from the curb. He felt like such an idiot.

"You can kiss me when we get home."

A hum vibrated from deep inside Enzo's chest. He really wanted to do more than kiss. Unfortunately, the last time they had sex, Enzo ruined Aric's life. He needed Aric to give him a sign. Enzo didn't want to pounce on him like a dog.

Enzo kept his gaze locked on the road, trying to kill his overwhelming lust. "How do you feel about visiting my club tonight? I haven't been by there in a few weeks."

"Clubbing isn't really my thing anymore. You can go without me. My feelings won't be hurt."

Since Enzo owned a club, he needed Aric to be willing to go with him occasionally. Cooper had given him the place. Enzo couldn't turn his back on it. "I'd really love for you to go with me. You could wear one of those sexy dresses you own, and we could slow dance. I could picture that." He really could. Enzo fought the urge to adjust his cock at only the thought of Aric dressed up and in his arms.

Aric didn't respond.

Enzo risked a quick glance his way. Aric had his head leaned back against the seat and his gaze locked on Enzo.

"What's wrong?"

At Enzo's question, Aric shook his head. "I don't feel like the same guy who used to confidently wear makeup and dresses in public. My life is different now. Plus, do you even own the type of place where I could safely go dressed that way?"

A shot of outrage raced through Enzo. He held the steering wheel so tightly, his knuckles turned white. "I'd fucking better. Let me find out anyone got hurt or bullied for being themselves at my club. I'll break someone's goddamn legs."

"You're sweet."

Enzo's shoulders relaxed at Aric's claim. "I'm not, but I'm glad you think so. We'll do something else tonight. I don't want you to feel uncomfortable."

"Right now, all I want is a shower. I feel so gross."

Enzo fought to keep his eyes straight ahead. An image of Aric with hot water running down his body fired to life inside Enzo's head. He had never wanted anyone this badly. "I'll make you something to eat while you shower."

"Let's order something tonight. You're not my slave."

Enzo steered into the parking space outside Aric's apartment. He looked Aric's way once he finally had the freedom to do so. "I have to keep busy, so I don't beg you to let me watch you shower."

A smile exploded across Aric's face. "I'd be too self-conscious to get properly clean. You could always wait for me in the bed... room," Aric slowly added, as if losing his courage to say what he really wanted. It was too late. Enzo had seen the lust in his eyes. He didn't have to be brave. Enzo had gotten his sign.

"We'd better let you get that shower."

With a nod from Aric, they headed for the door. While Aric tried unlocking the door, Enzo crowded his space and kissed his neck. His senses were on high alert. They were so close now. Soon Enzo would be inside Aric again.

This time, he wouldn't be forgetting a single damn second.

Inside the apartment, Enzo stole the kiss he really wanted while Aric tried making his way to the shower. Enzo kissed him all the way to the bathroom door, forcing Aric to shut the door in his face. A smile stretched his lips the moment he was alone. Enzo stripped off his shirt and moved to sit on the bed. Time moved slow as hell while Aric spent more than an hour inside the bathroom. When the bathroom door finally opened, steam rolled out behind Aric. His wet hair stood in every direction. If he noticed Enzo sitting on his bed, he didn't acknowledge him. The towel wrapped around his waist molded to his every line. Enzo's mouth watered. Aric headed for the dresser. Enzo couldn't let him dress. With his back to Enzo,

Aric's towel slipped to the floor. The blood left Enzo's brain and headed south. Enzo shot to his feet and pressed against Aric's back, letting Aric feel his desire as his arms wrapped around Aric.

Aric's gaze shot to the mirror above the dresser. Enzo met his stare in the reflection.

"I don't have any condoms."

Enzo slowly lowered his mouth to Aric's shoulder. "I do."

"Thank god." Aric's head fell forward, giving Enzo better access to his nape. Chill bumps rose beneath Enzo's lips as he kissed a path to Aric's neck. Aric smelled like fruit-scented body wash. His skin was still slightly damp from his shower. Enzo's cock leaked and strained against the inside of his jeans.

Aric reached over and opened the drawer beside him. He grabbed the bottle of lube from inside and set it on the dresser.

"I want you to be sure."

Aric didn't hesitate. "I'm sure." As if to punctuate his words, Aric's hand slipped between their bodies. He massaged Enzo's erection through his clothes.

Each breath Enzo took came harder than the last. He was so turned on, he worried he wouldn't make it to get inside Aric. Enzo needed to taste Aric's lips. He turned Aric in his arms. The lust and trust in Aric's expression nearly took out Enzo's knees. He had never been more torn between taking someone fast and hard and taking things as slow as possible. Enzo was desperate, but he also wanted to savor every moment.

He lifted Aric onto the dresser and massaged every place he could reach while he explored Aric's mouth. Enzo needed to feel every inch of Aric. He wanted to know Aric's body as well as he knew his own. The urge to taste Aric's entire body overcame Enzo. He longed to lick and suck. His ears craved Aric's moans. While Aric clung to the dresser, Enzo's mouth moved to Aric's neck. He bit. A needy whimper caressed Enzo's ears. Enzo's fingers automatically wrapped around Aric's cock. He stroked. Aric's short fingernails dug into Enzo's shoulders. Enzo's teeth scraped Aric's shoulder.

"Please?"

Enzo grabbed Aric's ass and lifted. His muscles tensed as he readied himself to toss Aric on the bed. A loud banging disrupted his plan. They froze. The banging didn't stop.

"Is that your door?" It wasn't easy to tell with the fan running in Aric's bedroom.

Aric didn't answer right away. They spent another second straining to listen. "I think so," Aric whispered after a moment.

"Who—"

"Open up, you shady bastard. I knew I should've called the cops on you last time."

"No."

At Aric's mortified-sounding whisper, horror raced through Enzo. It was Marco. Then the rage hit. "I'll take care of this." He set Aric on his feet and headed for the door. Enzo buttoned his jeans as his long stride ate up the floor. He couldn't believe Marco would show up like this. His twin had to have taken a two-day leave to even be here.

Enzo ripped open the front door and hauled Marco inside. "Stop fucking banging. Aric has neighbors."

Marco fought to push Enzo aside. "Where is he? Where is that little rapist?"

"What in the fuck?" Enzo had never been more confused, and that said a lot. "What are you doing here?"

Marco didn't calm down, but he met Enzo's gaze. "Danny called me. He told me you were hanging out with this guy every day. As soon as he described him, I knew it was that same manipulative bastard who roofied you last time, and here you are."

"You spoke to my boss."

Enzo's gaze shot to the bedroom door. Aric stood wearing a silk robe and looking so mortified, Enzo wondered if he would be sick.

Marco obviously didn't care. "Damn right I did. You already got away with this shit once. I'm not letting it happen twice."

The color drained from Aric's face. His gaze moved to Enzo's. "He told that story to my boss."

The devastation in Aric's voice and expression nearly hobbled Enzo. "Close the bedroom door, baby. I'll take care of this."

Aric took a step back and did as told.

"Baby? Did you just call that conniving fucker baby?"

Enzo's fist shot out, connecting with his twin's eye so fast, even Enzo didn't know what he had done until it was done. Marco flailed. Enzo hit him again. The level of satisfaction Enzo felt surprised him. This had been a long time coming and it wasn't all about Aric. Marco rallied. He charged Enzo. Enzo's fist shot out one more time, connecting with Marco's jaw. He went down.

Enzo stared down at his brother. They had been born almost identical except for the eyes. Marco's were green while Enzo's were hazel. They didn't look that much alike anymore. Marco had lost weight and still had his short military cut. Enzo had let his hair grow wild. At the moment, Marco didn't feel like his brother at all.

"How fucking dare you?" The question burst from Enzo in an angry growl.

Marco scrambled to his feet, looking shocked and enraged. "I came here to save you from yourself, Enzo. This guy drugged you and took advantage of you. I already had to carry you out of here once. For all you know, this guy could be a serial rapist, kill you in your sleep, or worse. He might trick you into marrying him."

The truth struck Enzo. He didn't know why he hadn't seen Marco for what he was sooner. Enzo had been blind for all his life. "I'm sorry, but no. You know damn well everything you just said is a lie. Aric has done nothing to me, except make me happier than I've ever been. You're the one who's hurting me, but not anymore. I won't stay miserable for the rest of my life to match you."

Marco's green eyes flashed with something close to hatred. "You may be a minute older than me, but I've always been the one looking out for you. Now I'm making you miserable? You're embarrassing yourself here, Enzo. I've got men who served with us, good men, calling me about you. They're telling me all about this nightclub you own and how you're eating lunch every day with this... whatever he is."

"You need to leave." Even Enzo heard the threat in his tone. He would tear Marco apart if he kept talking. Enzo had too much pent-up anger toward Marco for too long now.

A hint of sadness touched Marco's features. "What has this guy done to you? You're obviously not drugged this time. Are you brainwashed? This isn't you."

A bitter-sounding bark of laughter burst from Enzo. He scrubbed at his forehead. "You know, Marco. Before I left San Diego, I was miserable every goddamn day. I can't tell you how many nights I thought about ending it all. When I moved back to L.A., it was hard to find myself alone when I was so used to always having you. Now that I've been away from you for a solid year and I've finally found the happiness that's eluded me my entire life, I realized something monumental. You're the reason I was miserable."

As Enzo watched his blow hit, he hated himself for hurting his brother. His rage kept him from taking the words back. He realized now Marco didn't care who he leveled as long as he didn't have to be alone in his misery. Enzo wouldn't join him in the gutter any longer.

"Take that back."

"Go apologize to Aric."

Marco's expression hardened. "I'm not apologizing to a pervert."

Enzo didn't hesitate. "Then get out and lose my number."

Marco visibly wavered. "You're my twin, Enzo. How could you choose this guy over me?"

It amazed Enzo that Marco couldn't see the messes he made. "It's easy. One of you hurts me and the other doesn't. Unfortunately, it's not the one who shares my blood and face that treats me like he loves me."

"I love you." The hurt in Marco's voice couldn't be missed.

The fight went out of Enzo. "You just burst into my boyfriend's apartment and called him a rapist—for the second time. You talked to his boss, ruining his reputation at his job and likely getting him fired. No sane, loving brother does things like that. This guy is the one for me, Marco, and you're intentionally sabotaging things... the way you always do when you see me getting too happy."

"That's not true."

But it was. Enzo's shoulders felt heavier by the second. Marco would never change. He would never see his faults. "It's time to go. I have to clean up the mess you made. Aric absolutely can't afford to lose his job. Not that you've ever cared about anyone else." He urged Marco toward the door. "Don't waste another two-day leave on me. I don't want to see you again." No one knew how much that hurt. Since the day they were born, Marco and Enzo had been glued at the hip. Once upon a time, Enzo believed that was because they had been born best friends. In the last year, he realized it was because he was Marco's hostage.

"You can't mean that."

"I absolutely do," Enzo said with all the hurt in his heart. "I gave you a chance to apologize to Aric. You didn't take it. There's nothing left to be said."

Marco stepped outside and met Enzo's gaze. "I never thought I'd see the day when you'd choose a piece of ass over your brother."

A tremendous sense of loss overwhelmed him, but Enzo couldn't back down this time. "You're not seeing it now either. You're the one who made the choice." Enzo shut the door in Marco's face. For a moment, he stared at the white surface between his twin and him. His heart broke. Enzo locked the dead bolt and turned off the light. The symbolism wasn't lost on Enzo. He had shut the door on his old life. His future waited behind a different door. Enzo needed to go comfort the man who cared about him and always put him first. He didn't know how he would fix the damage Marco wrought. Enzo would find a way. Losing Aric wasn't an option. Enzo already loved Aric. Now he had to prove it. First, he had to make some calls. He couldn't let Aric end up unemployed and homeless.

♥ · ♥ · ♥ · ♥ · ♥

Darkness enveloped Aric. He could hear the mumbled voices in the living room, but the sound of the fan next to his bed made it impossible to make out the words. Aric didn't want to know. His chest hurt so bad he wondered if a trip to the ER, waited for him in the near future. In the month Aric had been with Enzo, he had gotten extremely attached to seeing Enzo every day. Aric just never expected the price for that happiness to be so high. At least, not twice in one lifetime. Marco had talked to Aric's boss. Aric's brain refused to move past that one detail. Aric couldn't go back to work on Monday. His life had ended again.

With every minute that passed, Aric's panic and stress rose. He stared at nothing, watching his life fall apart inside his head. Just like last time, Aric lost everything for the same man. Surely love shouldn't feel like this. At the thought, Aric's breathing stopped. He searched his mind and heart. It was true. Somewhere along the line, he had fallen for Enzo. Damn.

Aric closed his eyes and tried to breathe. He didn't understand how someone as amazing as Enzo could cost him so much. Aric took another breath. This wasn't Enzo's fault. He couldn't control what Marco did. Still, if Marco turned Enzo's entire family against Aric, what chance did they stand? Resolve sideswiped Aric and hardened his heart. No one would take Enzo from him. Not this time. He had stood aside and let Marco wreck him last time. Never again. Aric rolled onto his back and tossed the covers aside. He would take care of this once and for all.

Before he could jump from the bed, Enzo overcame him. Aric's heart tried racing into his throat. He hadn't heard Enzo coming back to the bedroom. Now Enzo was everywhere. His tongue stroked Aric's. Enzo's nude body molded against his. All thoughts of violence disappeared. Nothing existed but Enzo. Aric was on fire. He wanted to get fucked. His earlier rage had transformed into desire. He was pure need, burning for release.

Aric bit Enzo's bottom lip. "Fuck me."

Enzo went still. He stared down at Aric. "One of the few things I recall from last time, you told me to go slow."

A month was too damn slow for Aric. "Now I'm begging you to hurry."

Enzo didn't let him down. He shot from the bed, grabbed the lube, and was suited up before Aric had time to change his mind. The moment Enzo was back between Aric's thighs, Aric turned into a complete wanton. He pulled his knees higher, offering himself without a single qualm. Aric was on the verge of panting and pleading. His dick throbbed. Aric's mind was a mess. He was tired of behaving so no one would think badly of him. Aric wanted dick, and he wanted it now.

The wide, blunt head of Enzo's cock pressed against the tight ring of muscles surrounding Aric's asshole. Aric drew a steadying breath. Enzo thrust. A loud moan came from Aric's soul. He let go of his legs and grabbed the headboard. Enzo took the hint. He took over holding Aric's legs higher and pounded inside Aric. Skin slapped against skin as Enzo's thick, long dick rearranged everything inside Aric. It was carnal to the point of violence. Aric savored every painful thrust. The discomfort vanished the moment Enzo found the perfect angle. Cries, moans, and jumbled words ripped from Aric with no connection to his brain. He was in his feelings and nowhere else. The internal massage had images filling Aric's head. He wanted Enzo to do this forever in every position known to man. Aric wanted to get bent over a piece of furniture and he wanted to play with Enzo's ass. He craved to taste Enzo's dick while also sitting on Enzo's face. Aric wanted the world to watch him getting pounded by this completely sober man. Aric hadn't coerced Enzo. Enzo was hard inside Aric's ass because he wanted to be there. Aric would make sure he kept coming back for more until the entire universe understood this man belonged to Aric. Only Aric. Fuck Marco.

With one powerful thrust at just the right angle, nothing mattered anymore. A strangled cry ripped from Aric's chest as cum shot from his cock. Aric grabbed his dick and stroked, massaging every drop from his over-sensitized dick. He was wild with lust while riding out his orgasm. The cock in his ass kept moving and driving Aric even crazier.

"Holy shit. Goddamn." A sexy roar vibrated from the walls as Enzo's hold turned damn near bruising on Aric's skin. He sawed in and out of Aric, using Aric the way he wanted. Enzo fell forward and bit Aric's chest as he cried out in pleasure. Pride and possessiveness filled Aric like he had never experienced before. He felt special, but it was more than that. Aric felt like they had created a whole new level of intimacy that neither of them had ever experienced elsewhere. He didn't know how he knew, but Aric felt it in his bones. They would never find this anywhere else. This was meant to be.

· ♥ · ♥ · ♥ · ♥ · ♥ ·

With his ear pressed to Aric's chest, Enzo listened to Aric's steady heartbeat. He never wanted to leave the happiness and safety of Aric's arms. He was loved here. Enzo felt that all the way to his soul. Unfortunately, the longer he stayed put and the more his body cooled, the realer the night became. He had finally lost his twin. It had been a long time coming, but it still hurt way more than he liked.

Enzo's mouth opened, and the truth spilled out. He felt too safe with Aric to stay quiet. "Marco is an adrenaline junkie. He doesn't really believe anything he said to you tonight. He was just looking for some new trouble to start. His next high. That's why he couldn't leave the Navy. Leaving the Navy meant giving up flying very fast, very lethal fighter jets."

Aric lightly scratched Enzo's scalp, making his eyelids heavy. "His attacks feel pretty personal."

Enzo held Aric tighter. "I know, and I'm so sorry, but I promise they're really aimed at me. We were supposed to leave the Navy together, but he backed out at the last second. I know he thought I would stay too because I've always done whatever he wants to do. He's pissed that I found happiness without him. The day I moved back to L.A., he told me the bar idea would flop without him and I would be re-enlisting in no time. He expected me to crawl back. Then Cooper stepped in and Marco didn't have the same hold on me any longer." Enzo moved up onto his elbow so he could stare down into Aric's eyes. He needed Aric to see him and feel him. "No one has ever made me feel the way you do. I know it's a lot to ask, but please don't let Marco ruin us. If you'll have me, I'm in this one hundred and ten percent. I don't want anyone else."

Aric's expression turned hard in a way Enzo never expected. "No one is taking you away from me, especially Marco. I let him carry you away from me once. Never again."

Enzo claimed Aric's mouth. He needed to taste the vows on Aric's tongue. As their lips met, everything inside Enzo calmed. He swore he felt his heartbeat slow and his blood pressure drop. Enzo was at peace when he was with Aric. He had come home.

Chapter Five

♥

QUIET SATURDAY MORNINGS WERE Aric's favorite time with Enzo. Neither of them had anywhere to be, and they got to sleep in. That meant eight a.m. for them, since Aric was used to being up at five and Enzo still hadn't stopped living the military life. Still, it was three extra hours of sleep followed by a lazy day.

While snuggled deep in Enzo's arms on the couch, Aric spent the day trying not to think about Monday. Every couple of hours, Aric recalled the night before and terror seized him. He couldn't go back to work on Monday. For the past ten years, Aric had lived on edge, expecting any moment he would be attacked for who he was. Now the chances of that happening had quadrupled. He had to come up with a plan. Unfortunately, he had few options available to him. By four in the afternoon, all Aric could think to do was use his three weeks of banked vacation time as his notice. Then take those three weeks to job hunt while praying he found something that paid at least as much as he made now. It wasn't a great plan. In fact, it was likely dumb as hell and he would probably end up homeless. At least he might not turn up dead. He couldn't say the same about continuing to work with hostile homophobes after what Marco had done.

"You keep worrying at your bottom lip. Are you okay?"

At Enzo's question, Aric tried to stop thinking about everything. "Of course. I'm with you."

Enzo caressed Aric's hip, taking Aric's thoughts in a different direction. "You should know I won't let anything happen to you, but I can see you stressing. I could take your mind off things."

A soft pant escaped Aric at the suggestion. Enzo's hand was already on a slow path toward where Aric wanted him. Aric needed the distraction. Half an inch from heaven, someone knocked on the door. Aric shot from the couch. His heart leaped into his throat. He stared at the door, expecting the worst.

Enzo moved at a slower pace, coming to his feet like a normal person. He kissed Aric's cheek, somewhat soothing him. "Don't worry. I've got it."

Even though Aric nodded, he fought the urge to jump in front of Enzo and beg him to leave it. They could pretend they weren't home. There was no law that doors had to be answered.

Enzo checked the peephole. He tossed Aric a bright smile and hurriedly opened the door. "Cooper." At his happy cry, Aric tried to see around Enzo's huge frame to get a look at the brother-in-law Enzo loved so much. Instead, there was no missing the huge bull of a man at Cooper's back. His eyes looked just like Enzo's.

"I don't hear you yelling, 'Tito' because I'm your brother and shit. Nope. It's all about Cooper now."

Enzo stepped aside laughing, and Aric saw him. A tiny blond with light green eyes that flashed with mischief stood with one of his husband's massive arms wrapped around him, protecting him.

Cooper spotted him at the same time. He stepped inside, heading Aric's way without a hint of animosity in his eyes. "You must be Aric."

Aric nodded and held his hand out for Cooper to shake. "I'm guessing you're Cooper since Enzo yelled your name for the neighborhood to hear."

Cooper ignored his hand and hugged him. Aric realized too late how stiffly he stood in Cooper's hold. The embrace ended and Aric immediately over thought the entire half second of hugging. Cooper probably thought he was frigid or didn't like him. Great. Enzo's entire family was doomed to hate him.

Cooper didn't look the least bit put off by Aric's lack of response. He simply spoke a mile a minute, like they had known each other forever. "Marco said you're about my size. I'm so glad he was right about one thing. You can wear one of my suits. I figure it's been a while since you've done a job interview."

"What?" Aric dragged out the word, confused as fuck. He had no idea what was happening. The one thing Aric knew was Marco's name had been mentioned. He didn't like that. Aric fought the urge to say as much.

Tito stepped forward and handed Cooper a suit bag. "This should fit perfectly."

Aric looked between them, completely lost. His gaze moved Enzo's way. Enzo smiled like he was in the loop. No one enlightened him.

Cooper put his free arm over Aric's shoulders and steered him toward the bedroom. "I'm assuming this is your room. Let's go try on the suit and I'll explain."

Aric went because curiosity had him in its grip. He didn't ask any questions until the bedroom door closed behind them and he was out from underneath Tito's stare. Tito looked mean... and big. Aric didn't want trouble. He already had Marco against him. Cooper seemed more manageable. "What's going on?"

Cooper handed him the garment bag. "You have a job interview. Don't worry. You don't have to go anywhere. Baker is coming to you."

With the bag held to his chest, Aric didn't budge. He didn't know what to do or say. Everything felt surreal.

A sweet smile touched Cooper's lips. He took the bag back and carried it to the bed. "Marco showed up at the house last night, drunk and bruised. Tito was more than a little shocked to learn Enzo was the one who had beaten the shit out of him. I wasn't surprised at all. Enzo and Marco had been set to explode for a while."

Aric blinked. "Enzo beat him up. I didn't know. He told me to stay in the bedroom after Marco screamed at the top of his lungs that I'm a rapist."

Cooper paused in removing the suit from the bag. He looked Aric's way. "I can't even imagine. When he finished telling us the whole story, I wanted to come over right then, but Tito told me to wait until Enzo had time to smooth things over. I've never seen Enzo happier than he's been this past month with you. He never stops talking about you."

Aric didn't know what to say. He hadn't even known Enzo talked to Cooper that often. It seemed they saw each other more than Aric realized.

Cooper went back to his task. "Marco is unhappy, and—between us—I think he's a bit controlling. More than a bit. I think he might need some help, but that's a whole other story for another time. Right now, we have to get you dressed to impress."

Aric's tongue finally thawed, allowing him to speak. "I still don't understand the job interview thing."

Cooper handed him a pair of pants and Aric undressed on autopilot. "My attorney, Baker Cox, needs someone." Cooper paused and made a gesture as if searching for a word. Finally, he shrugged. "For a lack of a better word, he needs a lackey. Someone to stay attached to his hip all day, making his tea, running errands, and keeping him on schedule."

"A personal assistant."

Cooper snapped his fingers at Aric's suggestion. "Yes. A personal assistant. Since he owes me for a total dick move he made a while back, I suggested he consider you for the job. Because, let's face it, you can't go back to your job after what Marco did. You'll end up hate-crimed."

Tears sprang to Aric's eyes, and he dropped his gaze to focus on getting dressed. "That's exactly what I've been thinking all day. I think I've barely escaped ending up concreted beneath one of L.A.'s businesses for the past ten years. Now Marco talked to my boss." The bitterness in Aric's voice couldn't be missed. He was angrier than he could control.

Cooper rubbed his arm, bringing Aric's gaze back to his. He found understanding staring back at him. "It's okay. You have every right to be upset. Sometimes, life leaves you no other choice but to start over as someone new. That's why I'm here. Baker can be a bit stiff, and he pisses me off sometimes, but he'd be a great boss for you. He doesn't have a homophobic bone in his body, and you'd get to try something new. If you don't like this job, it'll buy you some time to search for something else."

A smile tugged at the corners of Aric's mouth. "You talk like I already have the job."

Cooper nodded. "I'm guessing you do. Baker fucked up really badly with me."

An unexpected laugh burst from Aric at Cooper's tone. He sounded like he had the power to change the world by asking for one favor. Aric liked him.

Cooper smiled. "See? Things are looking up already. Enzo loves you. Tito and I won't let anything happen to you. We like seeing Enzo smile. He didn't do it much before you."

While Aric doubted Enzo actually loved him, it was nice to hear. He let Cooper help him dress with that thought warming his chest.

Cooper buttoned Aric's shirt. "I think you and I are identical in size. My clothes fit you perfectly. That kind of makes me want to try on that dress you have hanging on the closet door."

Aric's gaze shot toward the closet. He forgot he hadn't put away the last dress he wore for Enzo in private. Aric refused to feel self-conscious about something that brought him so much joy. "I don't know how much time we have before this Baker guy gets here, but you can if you want."

Cooper's expression turned sad. "I'm not beautiful like you. The more clothes I have covering this body, the better."

Shock nearly rendered Aric mute. Not only was Cooper gorgeous, but he had also snagged a bodyguard almost as famous as the man he protected. Aric never would have pegged Cooper as someone with low self-esteem. "You're gorgeous. Why would you say that?"

A small smile touched Cooper's lips. He turned away and lifted the back of his t-shirt for half a second before dropping the material and snatching the tie from the bed as if he couldn't stand what he had just done. It took everything Aric possessed to stop his mouth from falling open. Scars covered Cooper's entire back—like he had been beaten daily with a bull whip.

Thankfully, Cooper didn't make him ask. He explained while tying Aric's tie. "My father was the devil. He ruined any chance of me getting to be pretty. You have beautiful eyes."

Aric couldn't tear his gaze away from Cooper's eyes. He realized in that moment he had met a genuinely good person. From what Enzo had told him, Tito worshipped his husband. That meant Tito was every bit as wonderful as the man helping Aric dress. Aric felt blessed to have landed in his company.

"Last night, when Marco showed up, I worried Enzo and I were doomed. I thought I didn't stand a chance with his family. That meant it was only a matter of time before he bailed. You have no idea how grateful I am you're here, giving me a shot. I love Enzo. I don't want to lose him."

Cooper set his hands on Aric's shoulders and squeezed. "Enzo is one of the best people I've ever met. Trust me. He can't be budged."

Aric truly hoped Cooper was right. He wasn't like Cooper. Aric didn't have the ability to call in favors and set people at ease. He had lost his spark years ago. All he had was himself to offer. Aric prayed it was enough because he hadn't been lying. He really did love Enzo. Aric wanted to be worthy of him.

"Thank you for this."

"No thanks needed," Cooper said, turning away to inspect the dress hanging on the back of the door. Aric moved to join him. He had lots of sexy dresses. There were at least three

Cooper could wear that wouldn't show his back. If Cooper wanted to borrow one to wear for Tito, Aric was down to help. He had a great feeling they could be friends. There was no time like now to get started.

·♥·♥·♥·♥·♥·

It was a little strange watching his attorney interview his boyfriend, but Enzo rolled with it. Baker would be a great boss for Aric. Since Enzo had partied with Baker in the past, he knew Baker was not only completely fine with everyone's various sexualities, but he also wasn't exactly straight either. Baker was attracted to whoever caught his intellectual attention. Enzo noticed things about people, and no one caught Baker's eye until they captured his mind. Gender factored not at all into the equation. Enzo liked that about him.

While Cooper, Tito, and Enzo stayed in Aric's bedroom during Aric's interview, Enzo kept trying to eavesdrop. It was better than seeing anything going on behind him. Cooper had shown Tito a dress Aric offered to loan him, and the next thing Enzo knew, the pair had disappeared inside the bathroom. Enzo didn't want to know. He needed to focus on Aric.

Ten minutes of Aric and Baker chatting turned into laughter. They were obviously hitting it off. Enzo tried to stay out of Baker's line of sight. He didn't want to pressure Baker, but Aric needed this job. He couldn't go back to his construction crew on

Monday. Danny was a huge homophobic bigot. No good would come of Marco's chat with him. Enzo feared Aric's physical safety was in the balance. He couldn't let Aric go back. If push came to shove, Enzo would find Aric a job at his club. He knew Aric wouldn't be happy there, though. Clubs weren't his scene. Working for Baker was the better choice.

"You don't have to hang out in the doorway, Enzo," Baker said, making Enzo realize he had known Enzo was eavesdropping the entire time.

"I don't want to intrude."

Baker waved off Enzo's concerns. "You're not. We were just hammering out the details of Aric's pay and benefits. He already had the job before

I got here. Dating you is credentials enough for me. I'm sure you're quite the handful."

That was probably true.

"Not at all." Aric's interjection surprised Enzo. He didn't stop there. "Enzo probably thinks it's the other way around."

Baker's steel-colored gaze moved between them. A slight smile touched his lips, as if a thought hit him. He shook his head. "I was just telling Aric that his lack of a vehicle is an issue for me. It's imperative he has the ability to come to the office at a moment's notice, as court can be somewhat unpredictable. I'll have a car delivered tomorrow along with a phone and credit card. Please buy whatever clothes you need to get started. The car will be yours to use as you please for as long as you're with the firm. Will that work for you?"

"Yes, sir."

Baker winced at Aric's response. "Please don't call me sir. Baker is fine. We'll be together a lot. Formalities get tiresome fast."

Aric smiled. "Okay."

Enzo couldn't look away from him. There was so much pride in his eyes that Enzo couldn't wait for everyone to leave.

Baker checked his watch and stood. As usual, he was perfectly styled. He didn't have a single brown hair out of place. Yet he still seemed frazzled today. "I apologize for my abruptness, but I'm playing tennis with a friend today." He held Aric's stare. "I'm thrilled to have you aboard. Enzo knows how to reach me. By the way, I was joking about Enzo being a handful. I know he's a good man."

Aric stood too and shook Baker's hand. "I know he is. Thank you for the opportunity. I can't wait to get started."

They exchanged pleasantries as Aric walked Baker to the door. The moment he closed the door behind Baker, Aric turned Enzo's way and covered his face with both hands.

"I can't believe that just happened."

"You were amazing."

Aric dropped his hands at Enzo's praise. "I thought a lawyer would be mortified I'm a dropout, but he didn't care at all. He seems great."

Enzo couldn't let Aric run with that misinformation. "He's a snake in the grass, but that's what makes him good at his job. Still, I feel much safer knowing you're with Baker all day than Danny and his crew."

Aric nodded. "Me too. I guess I should change out of this suit so Cooper can take it back home with him. Where did we lose Tito and Cooper to anyhow?"

Enzo motioned toward the bedroom. "I think Cooper is trying on a dress you loaned him. They're in the bathroom."

A bright smile lit Aric's face. "Good. I'll change too, and maybe we can convince them to go out to celebrate with us."

Enzo fought to keep his expression clear. "Um. I'd suggest my club, but Cooper has a problem with too much noise."

To his surprise, Aric nodded. He looked understanding. "I imagine that's true. My thought was something simple, like a nice dinner."

Cooper and Tito appeared in the bedroom doorway. "You two should come home with us."

At Tito's suggestion, Cooper jumped up and down like an excited kid. "That's a great idea. If you have something to celebrate, there's no better place to do that than with a genuine rock star."

Aric's eyes widened. "Are you serious? I can meet Hudson?"

Tito nodded. "He's always home these days. I'm sure he'd love to get to know you."

The happiness written all over Aric's face had Enzo willing to do anything to keep him like that. Aric had a job working for Enzo's lawyer. He was quickly becoming friends with Enzo's brother-in-law. In a matter of hours, Enzo didn't doubt Aric would be knee deep in attachments to Enzo's family.

Things were going exactly how Enzo hoped. One day soon, Aric would realize he was stuck with Enzo. Just the way Enzo planned for him to be.

Chapter Six

Aric: *I'm working late tonight.*

Enzo: *That's fine. I need to drop by the club and check on things.*

Aric: *Would you like me to grab us dinner on the way home?*

Enzo: *That sounds great. Are we meeting at my place again?*

Aric: *Yes. Please. Your place is so much closer to the office.*

Enzo: *That's fine. Se
e you later. Be careful coming home.*

Aric: *You too.*

·♥ · ♥ · ♥ · ♥ · ♥ ·

Enzo: *I miss you. Are you having a good day?*

Aric: *I miss you too, and yes. Baker took me to lunch and then had meetings all day. I've been chilling in his office, playing games on my phone.*

Enzo: *Free money.*

Aric: *Yep. The best kind of money.*

Aric: *I'm hitting the grocery store on the way home. Do you need anything?*

Enzo: *Just you.*

Aric: *You have me.*

Enzo: *Do I?*

Aric: *You know you do.*

Enzo: *We'll see.*

·♥·♥·♥·♥·♥·

Enzo's "we'll see" bugged Aric all the way home. After six months of dating, Aric was happier than he had ever been. Life was almost perfect. Sometimes Aric worried Enzo didn't feel the same. Working for Baker was a breeze. He basically only wanted someone around to do his constant bidding. That was nothing after ten years of hard labor. Not to mention, Aric often benefited from Baker's whims. Baker wanted coffee. Aric got coffee too. Baker wanted Aric to drive him to lunch while he finished a phone call. Aric got taken to lunch too. If Baker wanted to work from his yacht one day, Aric spent the day out on the water. It was great. But sometimes Aric missed the simple lunches in the shade with Enzo. They had started out strong. Now, sometimes, it felt like they weren't going anywhere.

There was so much going on beneath the surface. Enzo had a club to run. Aric never knew what time he would get home. Sometimes they were ships passing in the night. Aric hadn't been home to his apartment in weeks. They never slept apart, but Aric sometimes worried because they didn't get to spend enough quality time together. He never wanted to lose Enzo, but he wasn't sure Enzo felt the same. Neither of them had made any confessions of love, but Aric loved Enzo. He knew they would be fine.

At the grocery store, Aric picked up two bottles of wine and started making plans. He stopped by his apartment and grabbed a couple of his dresses before heading to Enzo's. Aric would tell Enzo how he felt tonight. It was entirely possible he was the only one holding them back. When it came to Enzo, Aric hadn't felt overly confident about them from day one because of their past. He needed to fully embrace them. If Enzo had stayed through awkward schedules and spinning wheels, he was in this for the long haul. Enzo deserved to see that Aric was in this for good too.

As Aric pulled into the driveway of Enzo's five-bedroom brick home, Aric's nerves frayed. He hoped he was making the right decision. The garage door lifted, and Aric steered the BMW Baker had assigned him into the empty spot next to Enzo's SUV. He grabbed everything, determined to carry everything inside in one trip. His stomach already shook. The last thing Aric wanted was to drag out his confession. Thankfully, the door was unlocked. Aric crashed through the kitchen, carrying his bag from the house, the one from work, and three grocery bags. He found Enzo at the kitchen table putting on his shoes.

Aric's heart dropped. "Where are you going?"

Enzo glanced up and then shot to his feet to relieve Aric of some of his burden. "I have to go to the club." Enzo stole a quick kiss as he grabbed a couple of bags.

Aric groaned. "Seriously? I just got home."

Enzo flashed him a sympathetic smile. "I know, baby. I'm sorry. They caught one of the bartenders stealing money from the register. I have to be the one who decides whether charges are pressed, but I want to question him first. If he's having troubles or something, I can't make it worse."

Enzo was such a great guy. He had the biggest heart. Aric couldn't be mad. "Yeah. You definitely have to go. It's just that I bought wine and I stopped by and grabbed a couple of dresses."

Enzo relieved Aric of the rest of his things and set them aside. "Then go put one on and come with me. We can make a night of it. Once I'm done questioning this guy, we can dance, and you can drink. I like showing you off to the world. You make me damn proud that you're mine."

Aric shook his head. "You go ahead and then hurry back. I'll make us dinner." He saw the disappointment in Enzo's eyes and rushed to smooth things over. "This way, I'll have time to shower and get really cute. We can have a candlelight dinner where we can both drink." He ran his hand down Enzo's chest, heading for his waistband. "Then you can ruin my makeup."

Enzo looked slightly less disappointed. "That sounds great, baby."

Aric's throat swelled. He had known it was only a matter of time before Enzo tired of him not going to the club with him. "Next time, I promise. It's just that you need to hurry tonight, and it takes time for me to get ready."

Enzo crowded Aric's space. "It's fine. Everything you said sounds great. And you're right, I have to rush out tonight. It's not fair to ask you to throw on a dress and hit the town when you haven't done that in years. I'll be back as quickly as possible."

Even as Aric nodded, he wondered if he had just lost Enzo. He felt an invisible wall erect. "Okay. Be careful."

"I will." Enzo's lips brushed Aric's. Aric clasped Enzo's shirt, trying to physically keep him from emotionally pulling away. After a short kiss, Aric's grip loosened, and Enzo backed away. Aric wondered if that had been their last kiss.

"I'll hurry."

Aric nodded and Enzo was gone. For a moment, Aric stared at the door Enzo disappeared through. He fought the urge to chase after him. His chest hurt. He was one thousand percent positive he was the one failing this relationship. Aric's shoulders squared. He couldn't lose Enzo because of his insecurities. That wasn't happening. If Enzo wanted Aric to be a part of his club, that was what Aric would do. It wasn't Enzo's fault Aric was like this. He needed to hurry. The last thing Aric wanted to do was miss him. He grabbed the bag from his apartment and rushed to the bedroom. If Aric hurried, he could be beautiful in under ten minutes. He would go to that goddamn club dressed the way Enzo wanted. Aric would show Enzo this relationship mattered. If it was the last goddamn thing Aric did, Enzo would know he was important to Aric. Whatever it took to make Enzo smile, Aric would do it. This was love. It was well past the time he should have said it. Damn the past. Aric could survive this.

·♥·♥·♥·♥·♥·

All throughout questioning the bartender, Enzo's mind stayed with Aric. Maybe he was being ridiculous. Enzo didn't spend that much time at his club, and it was his income source. He didn't go to work with Aric every day. Even Enzo wasn't completely sure why he kept pushing Aric. After choosing to pass on pressing charges and deciding to give his employee a second chance, he headed out to the main floor. His gaze scanned the nightclub he had very little to do with being a success. He watched couples dance and smile. That was what Enzo wanted. He wanted to show off his sexy man. Enzo never got to do that. It felt like their entire relationship had been in private. It was almost as if Aric was ashamed to be with him. Enzo wanted everyone to know Aric belonged to him. Yet he was always here alone.

Enzo scanned the crowd one more time. His gaze landed on a familiar face. He couldn't fucking believe it. He jogged down the stairs that led to the cash room and dove into the gyrating bodies on the dance floor. Enzo pushed his way through the throng until he came face to face with the mirror image of himself.

A bright smile lit Marco's face. "Twin."

Enzo didn't smile. "What are you doing here?"

Marco cupped his ear, as if he couldn't hear Enzo's yelled question, knowing damn well it wasn't that loud. "What?" He made a dismissive motion before

Enzo could repeat his question. "Let's grab a table so we don't have to yell." Marco snagged a blonde woman's hand as he headed off the dance floor. She gave Enzo a little finger wave as they moved toward the VIP section.

Once there, Enzo didn't bother finding a place to sit. "What are you doing here, Marco?"

Marco pulled the woman against his side. "What else would I be doing? I'm partying. Isn't that what people do here?"

Enzo fought the urge to pinch the spot between his eyes where a pain bloomed. "You know what I mean. You didn't tell me you were in town."

With a shrug, Marco focused on ordering a drink from a passing waitress. When he finished, he finally met Enzo's gaze straight on. "You told me not to waste another two-day on you. From what I understand, you're never here and this is an awesome place. I decided to visit the brother who still wants to see me and then enjoy a night out. So I'm here. You did good with this place."

Enzo didn't know how to feel. Mostly, he felt like a huge failure. He couldn't fix whatever was broken between Marco and him. Aric didn't want to be seen with him in public. Everything felt like it was caving in. All Enzo wanted was happiness.

Marco motioned toward the girl at his side when Enzo didn't respond. "Do you remember Georgia? I couldn't believe my eyes when I saw her here."

Enzo's gaze moved the blonde's way. She looked like every blonde socialite in California. Fake hair color, spray tan, and too much makeup. She was too skinny and probably never stopped talking about yoga, hiking, or the latest diet fad. Damn. He wanted to go home.

"Not really," Enzo answered when he realized they were still waiting for his response.

Georgia let go of Marco and leaned his way to speak against his ear. "Come on, gorgeous. You really don't remember me. Let me remind you." Before Enzo could guess at her intentions, she cupped his crotch.

"Think harder. I had this in my mouth while your brother fucked me the last time we saw each other."

Honestly, that really didn't narrow things down. Enzo moved to extract himself from the situation. Before he could take a step back, Enzo gaze met a set of beautiful amber eyes. The devastation that stared back at him left him frozen. Aric had on a white dress and adorable cat ears. People stared at him, waiting for his attention. Aric's stare never wavered from Enzo and the woman still holding his dick.

Enzo's heart stopped and then tried racing into his throat. His feet unglued from the floor and he took a step in Aric's direction. Aric turned away and speed-walked toward the door with his head down. Enzo rushed after him, but the crowd slowed him. It was as if men filled Aric's wake, chasing after Aric too—like they were fighting for their shot. Enzo fought harder. In the parking lot, he yelled Aric's name, but Aric ignored him. He finally caught him as Aric reached his car.

Enzo snagged Aric's arm. "Aric, hold up. Things aren't—" Pepper spray hit him in the face, choking off his words. He immediately released Aric and bent at the waist, coughing. His lungs and eyes burned. For a second, he wondered if he would suffocate. He coughed and choked. Enzo heard voices, but he was too busy fighting for his life to recognize them. Then the pain eased a bit, and he managed a steady breath. He heard his brother's voice and followed it.

"Sit down. Let me help. Holy shit. I can't believe Aric pepper-sprayed you."

Oddly enough, Enzo could. He knew Aric had fire. Not to mention, if roles were reversed, he couldn't say what he might do. Enzo tried to speak. The attempt only sent him into a fit of coughing again.

"Tilt your head back. Georgia found some water."

Enzo did as told, and Marco poured water in his eyes. His sight returned enough for Enzo to see Aric was gone. He clenched his teeth to keep from flying into a rage. Aric had finally shown up. Fuck. Aric was out there somewhere, thinking the worst of Enzo, and there was nothing Enzo could do. He was trapped in partial blindness.

Georgia practically danced in place at his side. "Was that your man? Did I just get you in trouble? Is this my fault?"

Enzo didn't know how to answer any of those questions. He had a bad feeling Aric wasn't his man anymore, and it was Enzo's fault. Enzo had pushed and pushed, guilting Aric into doing something he had told Enzo a thousand times he wasn't comfortable doing any longer. He imagined life was laughing at him now. Enzo had gotten his way, and now it would cost him everything.

·♥·♥·♥·♥·♥·

For two hours, Aric sat in his car in the mall parking lot. He didn't know where to go. His hands shook. The image of Enzo in someone else's arms wouldn't leave him. Marco had been there too. It was like Aric had gotten there just in time to witness Enzo's return to his old life. It was just as Aric feared. Aric had rejected him too many times. Of course Enzo broke. Who wouldn't? Aric was nothing special. Marco was Enzo's twin. That blonde chick looked like she belonged at The Aviator. Aric didn't belong anywhere.

His gaze moved to the rearview mirror. Dead eyes looked back at him. There was no spark inside Aric any longer. There hadn't been in years. The past six months, Aric had been pretending to be someone he wasn't. He never really stood a chance with Enzo. Aric had been fooling himself. He could never hang on to someone like Enzo. Enzo had probably cheated every time he went to the club without Aric. It made sense. That was why Enzo still hadn't told Aric he loved him, because he didn't. He begged Aric to wear a dress and join him because he knew Aric didn't feel comfortable like this anymore. Enzo had the perfect plan going before Aric broke and ruined it. He probably laughed every time he left the house without Aric. Poor, stupid Aric, falling for the lie that Enzo actually wanted to be seen with him like this. He was so goddamn dumb. Why would a straight man suddenly be desperate to be seen with a gay man in drag? He wouldn't. Aric had just so desperately wanted to believe it.

The anger was slow to hit. Now he couldn't feel anything else. He wrapped his rage around his heart like a blanket. Maybe he was an idiot, but he tried to always be kind. He wasn't to blame for Enzo's games. Enzo had chosen to cheat. Aric hadn't pushed him away. Fuck him. Aric never would have hurt Enzo. Enzo had no idea what he had lost. He would, though. It might take fifty years, but one day, Enzo would look back and realize he had lost the best thing that ever happened to him. Aric hurt all the way to his soul, but he wouldn't blame himself. He had been faithful. Enzo couldn't say the same. Aric just needed a plan to get through the worst. He couldn't go home. His apartment had too many memories. Plus, his things were scattered. A majority of his everyday belongings were at Enzo's. Aric couldn't go back there. He put his car in Drive and drove on autopilot. There wasn't a real plan in his mind. He just went where the car led.

After twenty minutes, the car pulled inside a private gate and followed a cobblestone driveway. The sprawling sandstone mansion looked oddly inviting at Aric's lowest. Soft lights lit the outside. Bright windows showed a warm, welcoming home. Aric parked out front on the circular drive. Perfect landscaping hid his car from view of the road. He didn't move right away. His nerves and emotions were frayed. Everything was falling apart.

The driver's side door opened, and the tears hit. Baker leaned in and unbuckled Aric's seatbelt. Without a word, he helped Aric from the car and pulled him into his embrace. Baker didn't ask questions or make him feel dumb. He just held Aric. Aric couldn't ask for more.

Chapter Seven

♥

EVERY NERVE-ENDING ENZO POSSESSED felt raw. He had spent the night texting and calling Aric nonstop. His texts went unanswered, and his calls went straight to voicemail. He had left so many long messages that Aric's mailbox was full. Nothing felt real anymore. He hadn't slept all night. Aric hadn't gone home. Enzo had driven by several times, but Aric's car never sat outside his apartment. He had this crazy image in his head of Aric wandering around town, trying to figure out where he had gone wrong. That was the best of the images. There was also a huge fear something bad happened to him. Aric might be in danger, and Enzo didn't know what to do. He wondered if he should call the police or Aric's family. Enzo had never felt so helpless.

Every time Enzo tried closing his eyes, he saw Aric's face. He looked like Enzo had ripped away every ounce of happiness they had shared, leaving Aric with his heart exposed. Marco was asleep on the couch. Enzo had tried to get him to move to one of the spare bedrooms. He claimed he wanted to be ready to beg Aric's forgiveness the moment Aric got home. The thing was, Enzo knew the truth. Aric was never coming home.

When the doorbell rang, Enzo damn near broke his neck racing to answer. He yanked the door open. As his gaze landed on Baker, he realized how ridiculous his race had been. Aric had a key. There was no need for Aric to ring the doorbell.

Baker didn't bother with niceties. He held out a key to Enzo. The one Enzo had given Aric. "I've come for Aric's things."

"You can't take his things." Enzo realized how dumb the words sounded, but really, Baker couldn't take Aric's things. Aric would need them.

Baker leveled Enzo with a cold stare. "I'm a solicitor. A damn good one. Are you really intending to tell me what I can't do?" Before Enzo formulated a response, Baker slapped the key and a piece of paper against his chest. "Along with collecting Aric's things, this is a letter of severance. I can recommend a few good attorneys if you'd wish, but I will no longer represent you or your brand."

Enzo eyed the paper. "What in the fuck is happening?"

Baker didn't spare his feelings. "I'm walking away from you as I wish I had done before investigating Aric for you. In my years as an attorney, I have represented many people I knew were terrible humans. After Cooper's father, I made a promise to myself I wouldn't do that anymore. If you wish to stalk men so you can humiliate them, you can find someone else to aid you. I have my own black soul to answer for when I die. I won't take yours too. Now, where are Aric's things?"

"This is my fault," Marco said, obviously waking up and overhearing the exchange.

Baker barely spared Marco a glance. "While I'm not surprised to learn you had a hand in things, I'm not really here to listen to anyone's confession. You two have gotten your revenge for what happened six years ago. Now it's time to move on. But for the record, you two destroyed a good man who didn't deserve this." Baker's icy stare landed on Enzo. "Even though I'm no longer your solicitor, let me give you some legal advice. You were damn lucky this time. Aric had me to come to after what you pulled. The next guy might try driving off a cliff, so cut the bullshit. If you have some sort of vendetta against gay men who like pretty dresses, playing those games could end with you being found criminally negligent, and I'd have no qualms testifying against the both of you."

Enzo couldn't believe his ears. "Do you honestly believe I took six months out of my life to trick Aric into caring about me?"

Baker's eyebrows rose. "You didn't take six months out of your life. You stole six months from Aric while you played at your club when he wasn't looking."

Enzo's temper shot through the roof. "I did no such thing. I love Aric. Last night was a misunderstanding."

"Aric's things, please."

At Baker's barked demand, Enzo snapped. "No."

Baker's eyebrows rose. "Are you really intending to make me sue you for their return?"

Enzo was too hurt and angry to care. "Yep. Sue me. If Aric wants to walk away from me, he can come get his things himself."

"Very well. We'll see you in court, then."

Baker let himself out and Enzo chased after him. "Will you at least tell me why Aric thinks this was all some elaborate plan to humiliate him?"

Baker paused at the door of his car. When he met Enzo's stare, Enzo realized Aric wasn't the only one he had hurt. Baker genuinely believed Enzo had used him to investigate Aric just to hurt him. "Aric doesn't believe that. I do. Aric just thinks you're a cheat who used his insecurities as a slick way to avoid getting caught in your indiscretions. He thinks you knew he would never agree to go the club with you. Aric thinks you laughed your arse off each time you begged him to go to that club, because you were pulling the wool over his eyes. He feels dumb and hurt because he fell for your bullshit."

"That's crazy." Even as Enzo said the words, he realized it probably didn't seem that farfetched to Aric.

Rage flashed in Baker's eyes. "Is it? Maybe you only think so because, like me, you know the real story. Like me, you know Aric doesn't know everything. He doesn't know you investigated him and stalked him. Aric doesn't know you planned to meet him. He thinks this is about cheating. I know better. Marco and you never do anything apart. I should've known this was something you hatched together. You make me sick. I told him you were a good man. You made me an accessory to this."

It was like getting punched in the chest. Enzo couldn't believe his ears. He felt like he was trapped in a bad movie. There was no way they thought him capable of something so twisted. "I love him, Baker."

Even Enzo heard the sincerity in his voice. Baker's gaze moved over Enzo's features, as if searching for the truth. Some of the rigidness left his shoulders. "I wish I believed that. In the very least, you cheated, and that's not love."

"He didn't cheat," Marco said behind him. "Like I said in the house, this is my fault. Enzo told me he didn't want to see my face anymore after what I did to Aric. Tito said Enzo never went to the club because it practically runs itself, so I figured I could check out the place and he wouldn't know. When he showed up and saw me there, he was furious and pulled me aside. The chick I was with came onto Enzo a little too strong. That's what Aric saw. He got there at the worst possible time, but that's the whole of it. Enzo did nothing wrong. It's all me. I'm the fuck-up. Bullshit follows me everywhere I go. That's not Enzo's fault. He shouldn't have to pay for this. I'm the one Aric should hate. Well, hate even more, I guess."

Baker's gaze moved between them. "I'm not the one you have to convince."

Enzo wasn't above begging. "Ask him to see me. I'll make everything better. I swear."

Baker shook his head. "I'm sorry. I can't do that. You already used me to find out everything about him. I have to live with that. That's as far as I'm going."

"Fuck." The word burst from Enzo at the top of his lungs. He had fought for so many years to be free and happy. Too late, he realized he had squandered his chance. Not once had he told Aric he loved him. How could he expect Aric to know it now?

"Good luck to you both," Baker said, climbing into his car. Enzo stood in his front yard, feeling like the world's worst everything, and there wasn't a goddamn thing he could do about it.

"Tell me what I can do."

Enzo glanced Marco's way before looking away again. He headed back inside. "There's nothing anyone can do. I lost my chance at being the man he needed. Maybe it's best I leave him alone." He didn't look to see if Marco followed him inside. Enzo went straight for his bedroom. He planned to pop a few pills and let the darkness swallow him. Enzo was too tired to keep fighting today.

·♥·♥·♥·♥·♥·

Since Baker had given him a sleeping pill around three, Aric slept solidly for ten hours. When he woke up at one o'clock in the afternoon, the house had been empty. Aric imagined Baker had some hot date or a tennis match scheduled. He felt a little guilty wandering through Baker's house unsupervised, but they were friends. When Aric had first gone to work for Baker, he hadn't expected Baker to be so amazing. He wasn't like a boss at all. Aric had things to do all day at work. It wasn't like he was always making free money, but Baker also talked to him.

Baker asked Aric's opinion on things and listened when Aric spoke. In no time, they had been exchanging life stories and spent more time talking than working. Aric had shown up here because he had known Baker would take him in. Still, he wished sometimes he could be the one with something to offer other people. Aric felt pretty fucking useless and unwanted. Some days, he wondered why he had been born. It seemed like his life should serve some purpose, but it didn't. He was just this oddball who didn't fit.

All Aric had to wear was the dress he had worn last night, a t-shirt Baker had loaned him to wear to bed, and a housecoat he had found in the guest bathroom. Since he hadn't known Baker wasn't home, he had wrapped himself in the plush bathrobe before heading out to explore the second floor of the massive mansion where he was staying. He found the second floor sitting area and a set of French doors. Aric carefully opened them, hoping he didn't set off any alarms. When nothing happened, he ventured out onto the veranda. It overlooked the pool. Aric leaned over the edge and spotted the garage to his right. As he looked on, one of the bay doors opened and Baker's black Cadillac pulled inside. The door slid closed and a huge Dodge pickup pulled in behind him. Marco climbed out. Even from above him, Aric knew it wasn't Enzo. They didn't carry themselves the same. Marco was thinner and cockier. Also, his hair was shorter. Not to mention, Aric had an immediate gut-check reaction that felt a lot like hatred at the first sight of him. Despite his hurt, Aric didn't hate Enzo. He worried he never would.

As Baker stepped outside the garage, Aric watched Baker's body go rigid when he realized Marco had followed him home. "What are you doing here?"

"I need to talk to Aric."

Baker stepped around him. "There'll be none of that under my roof. You've caused enough damage."

Marco stayed on Baker's heels. "Exactly. I've caused enough damage. Not Enzo. I need to talk to Aric and explain."

"You need to leave."

The rage in Baker's voice had Aric speaking up. "It's okay, Baker. I'll hear him out."

Both men looked up.

Aric clutched the lapels of his housecoat, needing to protect himself from Marco. He added an addendum. "From here. I'll hear you out, but you can stay right there."

Marco nodded and Baker went inside, leaving them alone. Aric knew that was only temporary. Baker wasn't the type to leave Aric unprotected. The moment the door closed behind Baker, Marco's gaze locked on Aric and didn't budge.

"Enzo didn't cheat on you."

Aric fought the urge to roll his eyes. "So now I'm a rapist and I'm hallucinating. Great chat."

Marco didn't look the least bit put off by Aric's rage. "You weren't seeing things. Georgia totally grabbed Enzo's junk, but he didn't instigate it and he was very unhappy about it. She was there with me. I like a certain type of partner. The kind who likes to share. Georgia didn't know Enzo wasn't single and Enzo was so focused on being pissed off at me that he didn't react quick enough to block her. As usual, everything is my fault."

To be honest, Aric didn't know what to think. He couldn't imagine Marco trying to fix things between them. "Why are you really here, Marco? We both know you hate me."

"I don't hate you."

Aric lost the battle against his eye roll. A tired-sounding sigh escaped him.

Marco didn't back down. "I'm serious. That night, at the Halloween party, I knew you were different. Enzo looked at you in a way he had never looked at anyone. I didn't like it. Enzo has always been just mine. I know how that sounds, but that's the truth of it. Seeing the two of you together had me drinking heavier than ever before. Then this guy told me he had seen you slip something in Enzo's drink and the two of you had left together. It was like I had been given a reason to attack you."

A bad feeling washed over Aric. "Who told you they'd seen me slip something in Aric's drink?"

Marco blew out a breath as if trying to think. "I don't know. It's this guy I've seen at a few parties over the years. I think we went to school together. Mike... no, that's not it. Big guy. Jet-black hair. Eerie-looking blue eyes— like a psychopath."

"Grant?"

Marco snapped his fingers. "Yeah. That's it. He said you'd slipped Enzo something, and he was pretty sure you two had gone to your apartment. He gave me the number and everything."

Aric saw red. "This whole fucking time, everything was Grant. Ugh." Aric took a few gulps of air and tried calming down. He swiped his hand through the air. "That changes nothing, though. The one time I go out on a limb for Enzo, I find him in someone else's arms. I hardly think that's Grant's fault too." He kind of wanted to blame him, though. Grant had a lot more fault than anyone knew. His eyes also weren't the only psychotic thing about him.

"That's what I'm saying," Marco said, bringing Aric's thoughts back to the subject at hand. "I'm the poison. Every time I'm in the picture, Enzo ends up taking the fall. That's the way it's always been. Growing up, if I did something wrong, Enzo took the blame. He even once took a school suspension meant for me so I wouldn't get kicked off the football team. I fuck up his life. He joined the Navy because that's what I wanted. Then when it came time to get out, I decided to stay, fully expecting he would just give up every plan he had for the future because I couldn't leave. I don't have a single doubt he thought he would finally be free once we went our separate ways. Then I kept showing up and causing trouble. Last night is just one more example of that. Please don't let me be the reason he loses you. Since the last time I was in town, I've realized I'm to blame. If he loses you—the only person he's ever loved —because of me, I'll never get my brother back. He'll never forgive this."

Aric didn't know if Marco was being honest, but he didn't think Marco would say these things to him otherwise. No matter what Marco claimed, he hated Aric. He wouldn't beg Aric to forgive Enzo for no reason. Aric decided to give Marco some fodder to see if he used it to strike out against Aric. That was the only way he could gauge Marco's heart.

"About a year after the Halloween fiasco, I ran into Grant at the grocery store. He said Enzo had paid him to attack me. Grant also said that he hadn't wanted to do it, but he was having trouble paying his tuition and he didn't think anyone would actually get hurt. He was pretty convincing. So I went to dinner with him, and we ended up dating for a few months. Long, horrible story really short, I ended up in the hospital and with a restraining order against him. It took me a long time to get over that. So no, Halloween night wasn't completely your fault. We were all ultimately set up by someone stalking me."

Marco shook his head. "That doesn't absolve me of anything. If anything, it makes me guiltier. I should've gone with my gut when I thought he was crazy, and tried to protect you. Instead, I ran with his claim and attacked the only person who's ever put my brother first."

Aric wanted to believe. He just needed to think. Things were kind of fucked up. "I'll think about everything you've said. I need some time."

With a nod, Marco took a step back. "I'm on leave for two weeks. If you have anything you want to ask me, or if you decide you'd like a free hit or anything, I'm staying at the Casa Del Mar in Santa Monica for the next week before heading out to Vegas. Baker has my number."

Aric nodded. "Okay."

Marco gave an awkward nod and climbed inside his truck. As he backed from the driveway, Baker stepped out from his hiding spot just inside the open door. He moved to a loveseat on the veranda and patted the empty spot beside him.

"What do you plan to do?"

With his bottom lip held between his teeth, Aric accepted Baker's invitation to sit. "I don't know. Everything happened so fast last night. I don't know what to think. Obviously, I want to believe Enzo isn't capable of this level of betrayal, but—honestly— dating Grant kind of messed me up. I don't trust people as deeply as I used to."

Baker draped his arm across Aric's shoulders and drew him closer. "That's a sentiment I completely understand. All I see is the underbelly of everything. I'm not sure there are any good people left in the world. Not even me."

Aric leaned into Baker's side. "We'll have to agree to disagree on that one. You've been nothing but amazing to me."

A bitter-looking smile touched Baker's lips. "I doubt that matters to the thousand people I've wronged in this lifetime." Baker winced. "But we're not talking about me. We're talking about Enzo. I went to see him this morning." Aric stared a hole in the side of Baker's face until he explained. "I returned the key like you asked and tried to get your things."

"Oh. I figured you'd just mail the key to him. You didn't have to do it in person."

Baker's gaze moved Aric's way and didn't budge. "Yes, I did. I needed to look in his eyes and see if he could do this. When we first met, I told you he was a good man. I had to know if I lied."

Aric's already broken heart ached. "You have zero fault in this. If Enzo created some elaborate scheme to destroy me, that's not on you. If he set out to fool me, no one is to blame but him."

For a moment, Baker stared at Aric in silence. Then his chest expanded on a deep breath. "I'm fighting myself on this one, love. He said that he loves you, and damned if I don't believe the cunt. The problem is, I can't be the one who ruins your life. If I'm wrong, and you take my word for it, I have to live with it." A sad smile touched Baker's lips. "I honestly don't know how many more sins I can carry."

Aric kissed Baker's cheek. "It's really sweet that you think you have that kind of control. Life isn't like that. I love Enzo. It's likely I'm doomed to beg him to take me back, even if he did fuck me over. I'm kind of lame like that."

Baker's gaze searched Aric's. "You're young and extremely beautiful," he said after a moment, surprising Aric. "I wish you would use that to your advantage and enjoy it. You only get one life. Someday, you'll wake up old and no one will ever look your way again. You'll become like part of the wallpaper. Don't let that happen without having lived your life on your terms. Trust me, being overlooked sucks."

A laugh burst from Aric. "I know you're not speaking from experience. You're incredibly gorgeous. I see the way people trip over themselves to talk to you."

Baker held his stare with his feelings hidden from Aric, as always. "I appreciate that. Would you like to go dancing with me tonight?"

Aric fought a smile. "I'm assuming you have a specific place in mind."

Humor flashed in Baker's eyes. "Not only do I know the perfect nightclub, I also know where you can find an adorable schoolgirl outfit. Sometimes, having deep pockets can be quite fun. What do you say?"

A nervous flutter in Aric's gut had him pressing a hand to his stomach. He didn't know if he was ready to see Enzo again, or what would happen if he did. All he knew was he loved Enzo. If he was about to lose him forever, he may as well show Enzo what he had lost and that he hadn't broken Aric. "How can I turn down such a generous offer?"

Baker brought Aric's hand to his lips. "You can't."

He really couldn't. Fuck. One way or the other, Aric was about to upend his life. He hoped he survived it.

Chapter Eight

♥

SINCE LIFE HAD A way of kicking him right in the ass, Enzo had been called in to deal with some minor paperwork issues at the club. He didn't bother looking nice or even brushing his hair. Enzo fully intended to get in and back out again. It was Saturday night, and the crowd was all happy couples or people on the prowl. Either way, Enzo couldn't bear the hope of it all when his entire existence felt pointless.

Enzo didn't make it five steps inside The Aviator before he spotted him. It mattered not at all how thick the crowd was surrounding him. Aric stood out like a brightly shining star.

The cat ears were back. This time, he wore a schoolgirl uniform Enzo hadn't seen before. Short plaid skirt. Tight white cropped shirt complete with tie. Holy shit. Enzo couldn't look away. At the center of the dance floor, Aric was completely surrounded by men. They pushed and shoved, trying to be the one closest to him. Enzo took a step in Aric's direction. The music slowed. Aric turned away from the men, trying to drag him into a slow dance. Baker blocked them and ushered Aric toward the bar.

Enzo shoved his way through the crowd, trying to reach them. He didn't know what he would say, or if Aric would even talk to him. All Enzo knew was he couldn't let Aric get away. He finally made it to the bar. Baker handed Aric a drink. His gaze locked with Enzo's over the top of Aric's head.

There was no animosity in Baker's eyes, only a silent warning. Don't hurt Aric again. No other chances would be given.

Aric turned away from Baker, laughing. With his drink halfway to his mouth, he froze. Enzo didn't speak. He didn't know if there was anything to be said. Instead, he plucked the drink from Aric's hand and passed it Baker's way. With nothing left between them, Enzo took Aric's hand and led him to the dance floor. He could feel the white-hot jealousy blasting in his direction as he towed Aric into his arms. Every man in the place hated Enzo for being the one Aric chose.

Their bodies swayed to the music. Enzo couldn't stop touching Aric every place he could reach, ensuring he was real. He pressed a light kiss against the shell of Aric's ear because he couldn't stay silent any longer.

"You look beautiful."

"Thank Baker. He took me on a shopping spree."

Enzo took a breath. He didn't want to start a fight. His words couldn't be held at bay. "I need you to know I would never cheat on you."

Aric didn't respond. Enzo closed his eyes and inhaled Aric's delicious scent to hang on to his sanity. It didn't work. "I've begged you a thousand times to come here. Why would you come here for Baker and not me?"

"I'm not here for Baker."

Hope sparked inside Enzo. "Why are you here?"

Aric tilted his chin up and met Enzo's stare. "I didn't get a chance to say what I needed to say last night. That's unacceptable. I should get to have my say."

Fuck. That didn't sound good. "So tell me now. You have my full attention."

"Okay. I love you."

Enzo dropped his forehead to Aric's. His neck would no longer hold the weight of Enzo's head. The mixture of pain and relief were too much. He hurt because he almost lost the best thing to ever happen to him. Enzo was relieved as hell Aric didn't hate him.

"I love you too."

Aric's hands went from being interlocked behind Enzo's neck to sliding down Enzo's chest. His eyes closed. "If I ever catch anyone pawing your junk again, there won't be anything left for them to grab."

Laughter burbled in Enzo's throat. He swallowed it. "Deal."

"You really hurt me."

The pain in Aric's voice nearly took out Enzo's knees. "I'm sorry. She grabbed me and the shock made me slow to—"

"No," Aric said, cutting him off. "My heart is breaking because we've been together six months and I was still able to so quickly believe you could do such a thing to me. Something isn't right between us. Something isn't settled. I don't know if we can make it if we can't figure out what's wrong."

Panic raced through Enzo. "I'll do whatever it takes. Just tell me—"

"The problem is me," Aric said, cutting him off again. "I'm insecure as fuck. That's not your fault. I've had bad things happen to me and I don't know what I need to feel safe."

Enzo knew. He was good at taking care of people. Protecting them. He wouldn't fail Aric again. "You look so goddamn beautiful tonight. I think all these guys will probably jump me when the slow songs end."

Aric rolled his eyes, but a smile curved his lips.

Enzo didn't stop. "I'm serious. They're like wolves around here. Don't worry, though. You're mine. No one is taking you from me."

Aric met his stare. "Never."

Pride swelled Enzo's chest. "Damn straight. I love you. I'd fight to the death for you."

Aric shuffled even closer and buried his face against the crook of Enzo's neck. Enzo held tight and moved to the music. He would make them better. As long as they were together, Enzo could slay dragons. Insecurities were nothing he couldn't handle. As long as he had Aric, Enzo would find the answers.

·♥·♥·♥·♥·♥·

Baker watched Enzo and Aric dance with more than a little envy in his heart. For the most part, his life had been wrapped up in building his firm. His reputation as a solicitor was beyond reproach. The rest of his life had fallen to the wayside. Tonight had been the most fun Baker had in ages. He felt good—like he had done a great thing. Aric and Enzo looked strong together. He didn't think Enzo had cheated. If he turned out to be wrong and Enzo broke Aric's heart, Baker would completely ruin him. There was no downside tonight. Unless he looked too closely at his personal life, that is. He was a tad lonely. Staying up half the night with Aric and then spending all day shopping with him, Baker realized how incomplete his life was. He would survive. Baker always did. He just wished he had what Enzo and Aric did.

"So you come with the sexiest man here, and then you watch him dance with someone else. Interesting."

Baker turned at the words. Seth Black stood at his side, leaned against the bar with a drink in his hand. Not a single blond hair was out of place. Seth was his usual self. Tall, trim, wide-shouldered, and perfect.

"He's my personal assistant, and friend," Baker added, so Seth understood he wasn't usually this chummy with all of his employees.

"Ah." Seth tossed back his drink and then set his empty glass on the bar. "That means you're free to dance with me, then." He plucked the two glasses Baker held from Baker's hands and set them aside. It was obvious Seth didn't intend to take no for an answer. Since there didn't seem to be any harm in one dance, Baker let Seth lead him onto the floor.

The moment Baker found himself in Seth's arms, his breathing changed. His heart beat a little faster. Seth smelled good. Expensive. It was nice. Seth was a doctor, and the smartest person Baker knew. That was sexy.

Seth's lips touched Baker's ear. "Have you been keeping that blood pressure under control?"

A laugh burst from Baker. "I know you're my doctor and all, but wow. That really made me feel old. Next thing I know, you'll ask if I scheduled a colonoscopy yet."

A sexy chuckle rumbled against Baker's ear, making it a little harder to breathe. "Nah. You just turned forty. I don't recommend those until fifty. Your blood pressure is my concern tonight."

Baker couldn't stop smiling. This was the oddest conversation while slow dancing at a nightclub. "I've been taking my meds, doc. Everything is good."

Seth's hand smoothed down Baker's back until he reached Baker's ass. He pulled him closer. "Maybe I could get your heart pumping a little faster, then."

Baker should have been uncomfortable. He wasn't. In fact, he felt more at ease than he had in a long time. "Maybe so." Even Baker knew he had sealed his fate for the evening with those two words. That was fine. They were adults. There was no reason they couldn't spend the night together with no strings or drama. No reason at all.

·♥·♥·♥·♥·♥·

Everything inside Aric was completely calm for the first time in a long time.

There were no voices in the back of his head telling him he wasn't good enough. He felt at peace. Being with Enzo was right. He trusted Enzo. Whatever happened in the future was out of his control.

The thump of loud music muted inside Enzo's upstairs office. Aric trailed around the room. It seemed odd he had never seen this part of Enzo's life before. His office was plain as hell. He had a small oak desk and a single gray filing cabinet. The only thing nice inside his office was his chair. It was wide and thick. Steady. Before Aric could comment on the lack of personal touch in his office, Enzo swept Aric from his feet and plopped him down on the desk. Enzo pulled his chair between Aric's thighs and sat. He removed Aric's shoes.

"So you don't run away."

With a smile, Aric tucked his bare feet beneath Enzo's thighs at the explanation. "I'm not going anywhere."

Heat blasted Aric from Enzo's aroused expression. "Good. I'm dying to know what's under here." He pushed Aric's skirt higher. Aric studied his every nuance. Enzo's cheeks flushed and his lips parted as he spotted the lace thong Aric wore. "Fuck. I have no condoms or lube or anything in this office, but I've never wanted anyone more."

"Your office is pretty sparse."

Enzo didn't look away from his under-the-skirt discovery. "I'm never here for long. Until last night, everything I care about has always been waiting for me at home." He ran his hand up the outside of Aric's thighs and hooked his fingers beneath the band of Aric's underwear. "Let me have these. I want to keep them."

Aric didn't hesitate to lift his hips so Enzo could drag the underwear down his hips. Enzo put them in his pocket. He settled between Aric's thighs again. Aric's desire grew beneath Enzo's appreciative stare.

"I'm hungry. Lie back."

The muscles in Aric's stomach clenched as he did as told. Enzo dragged him forward and licked Aric's cock. Aric slapped his palms down on the desk and held on. Enzo's mouth was so hot. Aric swore he felt every tastebud scrape his erection. Enzo left nothing unlicked. He sucked Aric's dick and balls while Aric writhed. Aric couldn't take it. He needed more. Aric shoved at Enzo's shoulders as he sat up. Enzo looked horny and desperate. That was exactly how Aric wanted him.

"Take your dick out."

At Aric's command, Enzo unbuttoned and unzipped his pants, setting his cock free. Enzo slipped down from the desk and straddled Enzo's lap. He kept moving until their erections met. Aric held them together.

"Look how gorgeous we are together. Perfect."

"Fuck. I really want to be inside you."

The anguish in Enzo's voice fed Aric. "Later. For now, I want you to watch my dick rubbing yours."

A ragged-sounding breath escaped Enzo.

An evil smile pulled at Aric's lips. He lifted and sat, moving against Enzo.

Enzo gasped. "Holy shit. That's hot. I want to watch you blow."

"Then don't look away." Aric had never felt more powerful than he did in that moment. Enzo's desire and reverence were almost tangible. Some things a person couldn't fake. Enzo's emotions were real. Aric felt worshipped. It was addictive. The lust hit like a freight train. Aric had planned to tease Enzo until they both blew. Now it didn't seem enough.

"Enzo." Even Aric heard the neediness in his voice.

Enzo's gaze lifted and collided with Aric's. For a moment, they sat frozen, staring at each other while the desperation grew. Then their passion exploded. Their mouths met, and they fought to get closer. They licked, sucked, and bit like they were starved for each other. Aric found himself crushed on the floor. Enzo licked his fingers before probing Aric's asshole. They kissed like they might not live to see tomorrow while Enzo fingered and stretched Aric's asshole. Aric scraped his fingernails down Enzo's body. His mind was gone. Enzo massaged the perfect spot and Aric flew apart. His cries vibrated from the walls while cum pumped from his cock.

Enzo didn't stop. He swiped his hand through Aric's cum and used it like lube. His thick dick pushed its way inside Aric's asshole and Aric cried out as a second orgasm hit. Shock had him gasping for air. That had never happened to him before. He hadn't known his body was capable of back-to-back orgasms. Aric couldn't breathe. His entire body shook. Enzo pumped inside him. In a matter of seconds, he cried out against Aric's skin, completely unashamed of his desire.

Aric's body turned to gelatin. He couldn't even lift his arms. His lungs fought for enough air to sustain him. Aric stared at the ceiling and struggled for life. He had never had his soul completely rocked before. Aric was a mess in the wake of it happening now.

Enzo stared down at Aric in horror. "Holy shit. I'm so sorry. I got carried away."

Aric couldn't formulate a response. He couldn't even catch his breath.

Enzo's panic visibly doubled. "Really. I didn't mean for that to happen. I haven't been with anyone else since the last time I got tested and everything was negative. Plus, I've never been with anyone without a condom. I'm a terrible boyfriend. I'm supposed to keep you safe."

Aric made a slashing motion, trying to cut off Enzo's panic. He finally got enough air to breathe. "Stop. I'm not helpless. I could've stopped you. It's fine. You're the only person I've been with in literal years. They tested me for everything when I landed in the hospital. After that, I was completely celibate until you."

Enzo went completely still. "What are you talking about? When were you in the hospital?"

It occurred to Aric what he had confessed while his mind was a mess. "It's nothing."

Enzo wasn't having it. "It's not nothing. What happened that landed you in the hospital needing to be tested?"

Aric didn't want to talk about this. There had never been any avoiding it.

"After I saw Grant again, and he told me that BS story about you paying him to attack me, we started dating. After a few months, I caught him texting someone else and broke things off. Two weeks later, he attacked me outside a nightclub in the gayborhood. He beat me, raped me, and left me for dead."

"Oh my god."

At Enzo's shocked expression, Aric tried sitting up. He felt too exposed. Even though he could tell that story now without choking on the words, it never got easier. Every time, it was like reliving a nightmare. Aric had to close his heart to keep from losing his shit.

Enzo snagged his waist so he couldn't get away and took him back down to the floor. He cuddled Aric so hard, he couldn't move. "I'm sorry I wasn't there to save you. I can't believe I've been begging for you to come here after something so horrible happened to you. It's my job to keep you safe."

Aric shrugged. "You can't save me from everything. Plus, it was stupid of me to believe anything Grant said. I should've run the other way the first time I saw him after that party That's on me." Aric turned his head and met Enzo's stare. "I'm sorry I don't trust easily or let people in. You deserved to hear every day how much I love you. I should've been saying that. I should've told you what happened instead of making you feel like I didn't want anything to do with this part of your life."

Enzo shook his head. "This isn't on you. I've never been in love before you. In fact, I've spent my life actively avoiding commitment. When I fell for you so fast and hard, I didn't know how I was supposed to act. I didn't want to chase you away by being as over the top as I wanted to be. I've been holding myself back, and we suffered because of it. My insecurities made you think I didn't care, but the opposite is true. I love you so much, I scare myself because I don't think I can survive without you."

Aric couldn't look away from Enzo. No one had ever exposed their hearts to him the way Enzo did. He was so brave, it was sexy. Enzo had handed Aric the ability to completely crush him. Aric would never do that.

"I love you more than life. You can't scare me." A random thought hit Aric. "Last night, before I got home from work, you asked if you had me. When I said yes, you said 'we'd see,' like you planned to test that. What did you mean?"

To Aric's surprise, Enzo looked uncomfortable, like Aric's question made him nervous. "Um, well, I got called away to work. That ruined things, but," Enzo took a deep breath, "I planned to ask you to move in." Before Aric could respond, Enzo fell into rambling. "I mean, I know you have your apartment, and you probably want your independence, but it seems crazy to pay rent on a place where you never sleep. Plus, it would just be easier to have all your things in one place. Truthfully, I'd actually prefer for you to marry me, but I know you'd say no to that."

"What makes you think I'd say no?"

Enzo shrugged and wouldn't meet Aric's gaze. He looked like he wished the floor would swallow him whole. "Before tonight, we never talked about feelings or the future. I assumed you didn't want to tie your life to mine."

Aric couldn't have that. "You assumed wrong. I'd marry you in a heartbeat."

Enzo's gaze shot to Aric's. "Seriously?"

Aric nodded. "I love you. I never want to be with anyone else."

"Wow." Enzo's tone held so much wonderment that Aric couldn't stop smiling. "We're getting married."

A small squeal escaped Aric at the sound of those words leaving Enzo's lips. He covered his mouth, trying to stifle his excitement.

Enzo pulled his hand away. "Nope. I want to hear your happiness. It feeds me." Enzo kissed Aric's cheek and chin before moving to his other cheek. "All of this is mine. I want more." His hand ran down Aric's body, hitting a ticklish spot.

Aric jumped.

Enzo leaned away. "Oh, boy. I found a hot spot."

A laugh burst from Aric. "No. Just no. Don't even think about it."

A devilish smile stretched Enzo's lips and Aric knew he was in trouble. He also knew in that moment that he would be happy. Genuinely. Forever. He had one hundred percent expected to get played the first time he met Enzo. Aric never thought he would find this happiness. Now he knew it was forever. He couldn't believe his luck.

Chapter Nine

♥

THE NERVOUS FLUTTER IN Enzo's gut should have been about something else entirely. Considering the changes his life had undergone in the past year, the last thing that should cause Enzo to panic shouldn't be going to see his twin. For the week Marco had been in Santa Monica, Enzo hadn't wanted to talk. First, all the horrible shit with Aric needed straightening out. Then he hadn't wanted to come up for air once he had Aric back in his bed. Aric was amazing in ways Enzo never dreamed could be his. But honestly, he had been using his love like a shield and it was time to face his issues with Marco.

As Enzo's knuckles skimmed the door of Marco's hotel room in Vegas, Enzo almost lost his nerve. He could go back to the room he shared with Aric and likely never see Marco while they were there. Marco probably had an orgy going in his room anyhow. He no doubt didn't want to see Enzo.

The door opened. Marco's tidy and empty room shocked Enzo enough to give him pause. He had genuinely expected a raging party to be happening. After all, Marco found one everywhere he went. If he couldn't find one, he started one.

"You know I was half an hour away for like a week, right? Leave it to you to go the longest route."

A smile snapped to Enzo's lips at Marco's dry tone. "Last week was kind of hectic."

Marco took a step back, silently inviting Enzo inside. Enzo stepped inside the room and tossed a cursory look around. Marco's room was the mirror image of Enzo and Aric's. A king bed, large bathroom, desk, dresser, and TV. Nothing incredibly memorable, but the skyline was gorgeous. Enzo snagged the chair at the desk. Marco sat on the bed.

After a moment of silence, Marco broke. "We're never going to be the same again, are we?"

The hurt in Marco's voice made Enzo's chest ache. "Nothing ever stays the same. That's life, but that doesn't mean we have to stop being brothers."

Marco nodded, even though he didn't look like he believed Enzo. His gaze met Enzo's and Enzo's hurt doubled. This had been his best and only real friend his entire life. Enzo didn't want to completely lose that. A sad smile touched Marco's lips.

"Why does it feel like we're no longer brothers?"

Enzo shook his head. "We just want two different things out of life. That doesn't mean we can't still include each other."

Marco looked away. "I'm sorry I ruined things with Aric. He seems genuinely nice."

"You didn't ruin anything. Aric and I are fine."

Marco smiled, but he still didn't look Enzo's way. "That's good. He's super-hot. I see what you see in him."

"He's also incredibly kind."

Marco nodded but didn't say anything.

Enzo pressed on. "Actually, he's the reason I'm here."

Marco met Enzo's stare. "Really?"

Enzo nodded. A shy smile pulled at Marco's lips. "He was wondering... we wondered if you would come downstairs to the chapel and stand up for us while we marry."

The way Marco's eyes widened was almost comical. "Are you serious?"

Enzo nodded. "You're my twin. I can't do this without you."

"Yeah. I mean, of course. You can't let this guy get away, so I'd be more than happy to guard the door so he can't run out screaming."

Laughter burbled in Enzo's throat. "I appreciate that. Aric can be feisty as hell. Sometimes he has pepper spray. I need all the help I can get." They were both smiling for once and it felt good. Enzo didn't want to lose his brother. His smile slipped away. "You're my best friend, Marco. I don't want to lose that."

"I'm not going anywhere. Don't worry. I'll make Aric love me."

Enzo held up both hands. "Whoa. Don't get too carried away. We look too much alike for that."

Marco's smile grew until it turned to laughter. "I've seen your bed. It's big enough for all three of us. We can just squish Aric between us."

He knew Marco was joking. Enzo had missed his brother's smile and laughter more than he could ever say. Part of him wanted to sit around all day, basking in the recapturing of their friendship. He didn't have that much time.

Enzo glanced down at his watch. "Well, if you're in, can you be ready to meet us downstairs in an hour?"

Marco looked taken aback, but he didn't let Enzo down. "Absolutely."

When Enzo stood, Marco did too. They ended up in a hug. Enzo's eyes fell closed. No one understood how deeply he loved his twin. It had been hell drifting apart.

"I love you, bro."

Enzo fought harder against the emotions overwhelming him. "I love you too. See you downstairs." Enzo swiped at his eyes as he turned away and headed for the door. For the first time in his life, Enzo felt like everything would work out. As he made his way down two floors, a heaviness lifted from his shoulders.

Soon enough, Aric would be tied to him for life. It felt like a dream come true. When he let himself inside the room he shared with Aric, he caught Aric still in a towel and nowhere near ready for a wedding.

Enzo chuckled at Aric's undressed state. "Are you planning to marry me today or what?"

Aric looked frazzled as hell. "I don't know. Am I? I didn't want to get dressed in case Marco said no."

Aric was sweet and Enzo got it. This was important to Aric. He didn't want any contention with Enzo's family. The thought of Marco showing up every few months to spread hate over their marriage didn't appeal to Aric. He wanted peace. He wanted Enzo to be happy. Enzo couldn't love him more.

"Of course he said yes. Now will you get dressed? We can't be late for our wedding."

With a soft cheer, Aric dropped his towel and went on the hunt for clothes. Enzo stalked him around the room. Hunger grew inside him as he stared at Aric's delectable body. He found himself dragging Aric back against his chest and stroking Aric's cock.

A breathless-sounding laugh burst from Aric. "I thought you said we can't be late."

With one hand still working on getting Aric hard, Enzo set his erection free.

"We won't be. I'm too turned on to last too long, but I've got to get inside you. Fuck. You're beautiful."

As Enzo bent Aric over the edge of the bed, he said his vows inside his head. He promised to love and cherish Aric as long as they both lived. But he also swore to always keep improving, communicating, and valuing the blessings he had been given. As Aric's tight heat engulfed Enzo's dick, Enzo vowed he would always protect this beautiful bond they shared. In his heart, they were already married. This was his happy ending.

Keep an eye out for the next Candied Crush, *Beautifully Healed*.

Please consider leaving a review at the retailer where you purchased this book. Reviews really help with a book's visibility, which allows me to continue writing more stories. Thank you, Charity.

About the Author

♥

CHARITY PARKERSON IS AN award-winning and multi-published author with several companies. Born with no filter from her brain to her mouth, she decided to take this odd quirk and insert it in her characters.

*Eight-time Readers' Favorite Award Winner

*2015 Passionate Plume Award Finalist

*2013 Reviewers' Choice Award Winner

*2012 ARRA Finalist for Favorite Paranormal Romance

*Five-time winner of The Mistress of the Darkpath

Connect with her online:

—Sign up for my newsletter: https://sendfox.com/charityparkerson

—Join my readers' group on Facebook: http://bit.ly/CharitysTribe

—Website: charityparkerson.com

—Facebook:
facebook.com/authorCharityParkerson
facebook.com/TheMenofSin—Twitter:
twitter.com/CharityParkerso

—Instagram:
Instagram.com/sinnerauthor

—Bookbub:
https://www.bookbub.com/authors/charity-parkerson

—Amazon   page:
author.to/CharityParkerson

—TikTok:
http://www.tiktok.com/@charityparkerson

www.ingramcontent.com/pod-product-compliance
Lightning Source LLC
Chambersburg PA
CBHW060312260626
47160CB00007B/2574